The Last Island

DAVID HOGAN

BETIMES BOOKS

First published in the English language worldwide in 2013
by Betimes Books

www.betimesbooks.com

Copyright © David Hogan 2013

David Hogan has asserted his right under the Universal Copyright
Convention to be identified as the author of this work

ISBN 978-0-9926552-1-1

The Last Island is a work of fiction. Names, characters, places, and
incidents are either the product of the author's imagination or are used
fictitiously. Any resemblance to actual persons, living or dead, events, or
locales is entirely coincidental.

Cover image by Stephen Walford Photography/Flickr/Getty Images

Cover design by JT Lindroos

To Ismini

PROLOGUE

The first time I saw the island, it was on fire.

Rocky, dry and largely barren, the island was dominated by a single forested mountain on the far side. From the top of the mountain, long fingers of flames extended into the sky. Two fat, manila-colored seaplanes buzzed overhead. Alternatively they landed in the water, filled their bellies, and took off to douse the blaze.

I watched from the bow of the ferry.

Darting images of the flames danced on the sea in front of me. The ferry chased these images to the pier, dropped anchor, pivoted and ground to a halt. Just ahead the ancient village stepped up the hill, a cascade of blue shuttered white houses, marked by tiny passage ways. To the left and right, a dusty road curved out and away. I slung an old duffel bag on my shoulder and disembarked into a heated breeze.

As I knifed through the small crowd on the pier, my pale skin seemed luminescent in contrast to the darker locals, who followed me with their stares. Almost immediately I was approached by one of those tiny widows in black mourning clothes who greet every foreigner with syrupy cookies and the offer of a cheap room. She gestured and I followed her up a cobblestone passage way through the village. The houses here were block-shaped, and almost every other one had a wired coop with a half-dozen or so chickens. Occasionally, there would be a donkey, ageless, thick-skinned and weary, tethered to a fence or wooden stake.

After a short time, the widow opened the door of an anonymous white house and led me to my room, an unadorned, cemented cube containing a bed and a wooden table. A solitary window on the opposite wall faced the mountain. The widow nodded, smiled and left. I plopped on the hard bed, inhaled the stale air of the room and viewed the fire framed by the square window.

For an unknown length of time this tiny Greek island was to be my home.

As I knew no one here and spoke the language imperfectly, paranoia encroached. I spent most of the night wondering if the place where I'd been offered a job – the Taverna Giorgos – even existed.

Despite my exhaustion I lay awake, staring out the window. Twilight slipped away and darkness embraced the island. Yet, on the mountain, the red of the fire and the red of the sun had merged – and, there, the final moment of day had been stilled into a sort of vigil for the coming dawn. I stared at the unceasing glow, stirred into a dry-eyed regret, and listened to the drone of the planes echo against the bare walls of my room. In time, the planes departed into the moonless night.

But the fire survived – as I, too, once did.

In the morning, the fishermen, store owners, wives and children of the island emerged from their white houses and shuffled into daily life. Without exception, they ignored the fire, unaffected by the acrid air and the pall of black smoke over the mountain.

And, somehow, this seemed so right that I felt I was fated for the island. For what better than a place where fire is ignored – where an isolated people discount the very thing threatening to destroy them? What better than a place where life is pared down to the core – fishing, eating, sleeping? For if there was a large part of myself that had to be pared away, if I, too, had to be burned down to the essence, could there be a better place than this distant and simple island to do so?

It was likely that I was just talking myself into it, however, because the truth was that for a hapless pilgrim like myself – a friendless, penitent, former Boston firefighter – there was, in fact, nowhere else to go.

1

I was famished the morning after my arrival and went in search of food. It wasn't easy. The dirt and cobblestone passageways that led to the harbor were an inscrutable maze and so narrow that many times I could spread my arms and touch the houses on both sides. After the initial morning bustle, the island had come to a standstill. The only people who remained were old women, shaking blankets from balconies, sweeping dirt from doorsteps or dumping buckets of water down the inclined walkways. They watched me carefully as I passed by, curious and suspicious about the stranger in their midst.

After some time and many wrong turns, I reached the harbor and found a small grocery store. I pointed to a crusted, triangular pastry under the plastic counter for my breakfast and then ordered coffee. The bemused young girl behind the counter gave me the pastry and then poured cold water into a plastic cup, dumped in some coffee granules and shook it. I took my pastry and coffee outside and sat on the curb, staring at the vacant harbor quivering under the rising sun. The coffee was watery and tasteless, and the pastry stuffed with a piquant goat cheese that was far too strong for breakfast, but I'd not eaten in more than twelve hours and wolfed it down.

My stomach satisfied, I looked about at what was to be my new home. It wasn't much. In addition to the store where I'd bought my coffee, the village consisted of no more than a tiny bank, soccer field, three empty storefronts and two tavernas situated on opposite sides of the harbor, one with green trim and one with blue. One of these had to be the Taverna Giorgos, I thought, or else I'd come to the wrong place – a possibility as likely as any other.

I guessed right – it was a fifty-fifty chance, after all – and went to the blue trimmed taverna first, where Mr. Giorgos, a thick-set and energetic man who spoke heavy English, acted as if he'd been expecting me. We'd met on the deck of a passenger ship to Morocco – a destination I'd chosen because, more than anything else, it sounded exotic and remote. I'd been eating pickled eels from a can, and he'd been sipping whiskey from the bottle. The two seemed like a good combination, and I offered to trade.

We fell into conversation, and when he learned that I spoke some Greek, he mentioned that he was looking for help at his taverna. He wanted to travel more, he said, and all of the local men fished and weren't interested in low pay waiter work. Of course, there was no way to gauge how serious he was about an offer shouted over whiskey and eels as a cruel Moroccan wind whipped at our ears. But weary from my travels and, perhaps because a man without a destination is always seeking one, even against his better judgment, I decided to come to the island anyway. Now, in the stifling heat of the taverna, Mr. Giorgos tested my knowledge of Greek beverages – *beera, ouzo, retsina, krassi* – and then put me to work behind the bar, simple as that.

The Taverna Giorgos was a small and simple place, a stripped down fisherman's watering hole, though its aspirations at one time may have been better. Rusted 'Stella Artois',

'Guinness', and 'Heineken' signs were displayed behind the bar, though none of these brands were available. A dusty, dartless dart board hung crookedly against one wall. Toward the back, a thin white counter faced twenty or so rickety wooden tables, scattered haphazardly, and surrounded by low chairs with poorly woven seats.

The taverna served coffee, soda, Greek wine, ouzo, beer and counterfeit whiskeys. Occasionally, fish (*psari*) or octopus (*octopothia*) would be available, Mr. Giorgos told me, when a fisherman offered it as payment for a tab. This was rare though, he added, and nothing for me to worry about – which I wasn't particularly, not quite comprehending why fishermen would buy fish in the first place. Ultimately, the taverna struck me as a hollow and elemental place wholly dedicated to its dual purposes: gathering and drinking. You could, I suppose, call it genuine.

I'd been employed for no more than a few hours when I met Martin McVie, the Irishman. He was sitting at a table with two Greek fishermen and Mr. Giorgos, playing cards. Martin and Mr. Giorgos were teamed against the two fishermen, one quite fat and the other with one arm. The game and the Greek were getting fast and heated when Martin glanced my way.

"*Beera*," he barked.

As I walked over with it, he looked at me again and said in English, "You sure as hell aren't Greek."

"American."

"Well, hey, hey, hey," he said, returning to the card game.

Martin was tall and thin, maybe fifty-five years old, with a hard lined face permanently reddened by drink and sun. Wearing ripped shorts, black canvas high-top sneakers and a ripped Irish hurling shirt, he looked like something out of a bad pirate movie. He had a hideous scar on his left knee, which he bent with difficulty, and there was some writing on his ripped, green fishing hat that was so faded it couldn't be read.

Martin spoke Greek fluently but reserved his frequent swears for English – whether this was for his sake or the fishermen, I wasn't sure. As time went on, the game grew more intense, and both teams began spitting curses from the four sides of the table. Suddenly, the fisherman with one arm yelled at the fat one. Then Mr. Giorgos slammed a card on the table, jumped up and kissed Martin on the lips.

"*Opah!*"

Abruptly, the two angry fishermen stalked out the door without another word, the one-armed man slamming the front door into the rear of the fat one as they departed. "Two beers," Martin called to me over the noise, "one for you."

I brought three beers to the table, and Martin said, "That's three beers."

"It is, yes," I replied, almost adding, 'thank you for counting,' but thinking better of it.

"I said two beers."

"You said, 'two beers and one for yourself.' That's three."

"No, I said, 'two beers, one for you.' No *and*. The American is stealin' from Giorgos on his first day?"

"It's a misunderstanding."

"Everythin' is." He stared at me as if looking for some clue as to who I was, and why, like him, I'd ended up here. I stared out the window and decided to wait him out. It didn't take long.

"Okay, I'll bite," he said, "Go on. Tell me what a pasty, devil-eyed bastard like you is doing on this God and beast forsaken island." I pulled out the chair vacated by the one-arm fisherman and sat down as he continued, "Was it a spiritual or psychological misadventure brought you round? Think of me as kindly Father Martin, your confessor, or confessee, or confessoree. Mary, Joseph, I'm forgettin' my English – not that it was needed 'til you came. So, was it desperation or eccentricity that brought you? Something lugubrious? Good word there, haven't a clue what it means. Goin' to answer anytime soon?"

"I'm waiting for you to finish."

"I have."

I took some time to think about it. It was delicate matter, one I wanted to approach tangentially, if at all. "I came here because I did too much," I said slowly, "or too little, depending on your point of view." A warm breeze wafted in from the doorway and felt cold against the sweat on my neck and arms.

"Jaysus, Giorgos, the hell'd you get this one?" Martin called to Giorgos before gulping the last of his first beer.

"The ferry." Mr. Giorgos said. "To Morocco, or from Morocco, I forget."

"Told you not to be goin' there in the first place. You know you just can't be lettin' anyone come in here and run the place. 'Specially a Yank." Martin turned to me. "Speak Greek?"

"Some. My grandmother was Greek."

Martin nodded, but was already thinking about something else. The two of us fell silent and drank our beers. Neither Martin nor Mr. Giorgos appeared to be in any rush to discover anything further about me. There would be plenty of time for that, I thought, for right then, sipping a warm afternoon beer during the long, baked, siesta hours of the island, it felt like there would be time for everything.

I wasn't sure that I liked the idea of this Irishman who, on the face of it anyway, appeared to have found a home here. It conflicted with my intention of being the only foreigner on the island. (The fact that I didn't know this was my intention until I met Martin only increased my disaffection.) It was as if he'd found me out in some way, and I resented it.

A few minutes later, Martin's second beer was half gone. Mr. Giorgos started to walk out the front door of the taverna.

"Wait," Martin called to Mr. Giorgos and pointed to me. "Tell him."

"What?" Mr. Giorgos said.

"He works for me. As well as you. Tell him he's workin' for me."

Mr. Giorgos inspected me slowly and then, as if condemning me, said, "You are working for him."

Martin turned to me. "Job description. Drink beer with me. Nod when you don't understand me. Shake your head when you do. Know that just because you speak the language of the oppressor, I haven't dismissed you out of hand yet. Time for that later."

With that Martin McVie, Irishman, guzzled the last of his beer and got up from the table. He limped to the front door, favoring his left leg, and stopped next to the mirror with the Tuborg logo. He stared into the mirror, whistled a few bars of a snappy Irish tune and cocked his head. Then he stopped whistling, took a deep breath and screamed. When he stopped screaming, he turned to me, smiled, and left the bar.

Mr. Giorgos was the most absent and carefree owner of any business I'd ever known. Over the next five days, he stopped by twice. The first time he took me around the taverna and told me how to open the front door (push in hard and pull up, no key required), where the money goes (an old shoe box), and how to pour cheap whiskey into expensive bottles (squatting behind the counter where no one can see). The second time he and a large red-bearded fisherman got drunk on retsina.

That was all.

Mr. Giorgos never told me how to mix any drinks or how to clean the glasses and tables and floors. Perhaps he assumed I'd been a waiter or a bartender in the States. This wasn't true, of course, but I saw no reason to dissuade him at this point.

The taverna opened every day around noon (at least, I *assumed* it did - no one ever told me), though most of the fishermen arrived about three hours later. The harbor lay just outside the front door, across the dusty road. In the afternoons, I'd watch the humble wooden boats putter in, one after the other. As soon as they tied up, the fatigued, leather-skinned fishermen would sort their meager, sometimes tragic, catches into buckets or trays and place them on the dock. Then the daily ritual of buying, selling and trading would begin, during which time the young kids, who played soccer waiting for the boats to arrive, jumped on their father's boats to clean the nets. It was only after the final fish was sold that the fishermen would begin filing into the taverna.

The men were a haggard bunch, crusty, unshaven, reeking of fish and oil. They argued, burped, and spit, their language and manners as coarse as their hands, which resembled the stubs of rotted tree branches. No one talked to me at first, just glanced once or twice my way when calling out a drink order. I, too, said nothing. My grandmother had insisted on speaking Greek to me as a child, and it came back quickly. Though it took me awhile to catch on to the specific dialect, I found I could follow the general trend of the conversations.

The fishermen were a close, strong-willed group facing, as bravely as they could, an untenable situation: their sea, the once bountiful Aegean Sea, was running out of fish. They joked among themselves in a rousing fashion, punctuated by

sudden gestures and hard slaps. But they knew that their lifestyle, and the lifestyle of a hundred generations before them,
was disappearing, and this fact seemed to haunt every conversation. Few of their children fished – the older ones had taken
jobs on ships or tourist islands or had moved to the mainland
– and so the old stories went unheard, the ancient wisdom
dying with the men.

They drank Greek coffee, ouzo, beer, retsina and bad
whiskey, while they played backgammon and cards. When
the talk did turn away from the wanting sea, it usually turned
to local gossip and age old rivalries: a pregnant daughter, feud-
ing cousins, the bestial tendencies of the next island.

The days rolled on this way, one identical to the next:
bright white day following bright white day; game following game; drink following drink. I walked the village streets
during the day, swam occasionally in the oily harbor water,
worked at the taverna in the afternoons and nights, and fell
asleep at the widow's house. I hadn't seen Mr. Giorgos for an
entire week when he walked in, marched behind the bar and
checked the shoe box. There was a significant sum of money
in it, at least, I assumed, by island standards, and he counted
it solemnly.

"Two days go by," he said, "and you give the money to
Savvas in the bank over there. He knows what to do." He
pointed outside to the only bank in the village. "I am leaving for a while. Going to Italy. You give all the money to the
bank. I take care of you later."

"When are you coming back?"

"I don't know. You talk to Martin. He will answer your
questions."

And with that, incredibly, the taverna was left to me.

"Where you stayin'?" Martin asked me the next day at the taverna.

I told him about the tiny widow.

"She with Giannopoulos or Papakakis?"

"Don't know."

"Hope she's not with Papakakis."

"Why's that?"

"You're with Giannopoulos."

"I didn't know that."

"Doesn't matter, you are."

I looked about the taverna and saw the fishermen as the intrepid, doomed warriors they were. Grown where planted, they were the opposite of me, with circumstances so alike that it seemed they could swap lives with one another – one boat, one house, one wife for another – and nothing much would change for anyone. I envied their rootedness and figured if they were Giannopoulos, whoever he was, that was good enough for me.

"Tell me about this Giannopoulos," I said to Martin.

"He's tryin' to *preserve* the Reserve, but don't be soddin' your American brain with that now. Be findin' about all that soon enough. Thing to be thinkin' about is where you're stayin'. Your flat doesn't sound like much fun, 'less there's somethin' about that little widow I'm missin'."

"She gives me cookies," I said, and noticing Martin's sly smile, added. "The kind you eat."

"Yeah, sure. But what about a sunny villa on the leeward side, replete with ocean views, full amenities, convenient to recreation and public transportation? Cheap, too, and with a subject of interest."

"What's a subject of interest?"

"Woman about your age. Australian and kind of pretty too, if you go for that kind of thing."

"What kind?"

"The kind-of-pretty kind of thing."

"Not interested."

"Yeah, sure. I do know where you be gettin' your cookies."

"Martin –"

"– The land is owned by an Animal Society, or some group that was here a few years ago. They want to rent it out, make some money out of it, and that's where you'd be comin' in." I didn't know what to make of this offer and thought it might be a joke. There seemed to be a trace of insincerity in everything Martin said, though that may have been nothing more than the Greek intonation he'd picked up, the slight upward inflection at the end of every sentence.

"Harry over there is the local real estate agent," he said, "Far as I know, he's listed every house that's ever been for sale here, somethin' which happens every couple decades or so. I'll go talk to him."

Harry was the fat fisherman who had been playing cards against Martin and Mr. Giorgos that first day. When he screamed at the one-armed man that first day, I'd figured him as impulsive and hot-tempered, and subsequently avoided him as best I could. But now as I watched him, it looked as if I might've gotten it wrong. He talked calmly with Martin, nodding his head and smiling with dingy, crooked teeth. They called the one-armed man over. He also nodded his head as they talked to him, and then Martin returned to me.

"You're in," he said. "They just wanted to know what crime you'd committed, figurin' you had to be on the run from somethin'."

"What'd you tell them?"

"You're CIA."

"If I was CIA, why would I come here?"

"Wrong question."

"And the right one is?"

"Why wouldn't you?"

As with so much else that Martin said, I found there was no real response. Martin was pleased with himself and squinted into the bright sun for a long time. "See the place?" he said eventually.

"Duty calls." I said, gesturing to the fishermen, who were drinking and playing backgammon.

Martin looked about the taverna. "No duty here. They'll take care of the place. What would they steal anyway? Where would they go? And what would they do when they got there? Besides, you work for me, and I order you to leave this taverna and go see the villa, or I'll dock your wages."

"I don't make enough for it to matter."

"Put a bottle of ouzo out and I'll pay for it."

When I opened the ouzo, Martin asked the fishermen to keep track of who drank how much and they laughed. Seconds later, I left the taverna with Martin and the two fishermen.

"Met these guys?" Martin asked as we walked down the dusty road.

I shook hands with both of them. Harry, the fat one, smiled at me with brown teeth, and Ari, the one-armed man, twisted his left hand over to shake with my right. Then the four of us squeezed into a tiny, rusted Fiat. Martin and I stuffed ourselves into the back, our knees wedged against the front seats in such a way that our feet didn't hit the floor. Martin winced as he pulled his scarred left knee into position but made no sound. Ari sat in the driver's side and put the key into the ignition by looping his left arm through the wheel.

"*En-ah,*" Ari said.

From the passenger side, Harry shifted into first gear with his left hand. There was a pause before the car pulled away.

As we started moving, a warm, dusty draft rose up from the floor. I looked down between my feet and could see the road speeding by through the rusted, golf-ball sized holes in the floorboard.

"*Thee-oh*," Ari said looking straight ahead. Harry pulled the stick shift back into second gear, and we followed the dusty road out of the village. The road thinned, and we headed through a flattened area to the other side of the village, the mountain hovering majestically to our right.

"*Tree-ah*," Ari said.

Harry pushed the stick up, but the gears ground resistance. Harry looked wryly at Ari and pushed hard again. The gears screeched frightfully.

"*Tree-ah, TREE-AH!*" Ari screamed along with a stream of unintelligible words.

Harry took his hand off the gearshift and abruptly smacked Ari in the head. Ari screamed at him, reached his arm clear across his body and smacked Harry right back. But Harry was fast; he grabbed Ari's arm and wouldn't let go. Miraculously, Ari managed to stop the car just as Harry took his other free hand and slapped the defenseless Ari twice on the forehead. Ari tugged his arm back and got out of the car. Harry got out the other side. The fishermen yelled from opposite sides of the car. After a minute or two of rapid-fire Greek they got back in.

"*En-ah*," Ari said quietly, "*Thee-oh . . . Tree-ah . . .*"

We headed down the road, winding now, and then turned down a rocky, unpaved path lined by trees on both sides. The path thinned as we went. We stopped when the trees scraped the car on both sides simultaneously. About twenty yards ahead, the trees wrapped themselves into a dark tunnel with a single beam of light emerging through the small opening. Martin, Harry and I got out of the car. Ari waited behind.

Knocking the branches aside, we proceeded through the tunnel.

On the other side was a small cove that looked out at the open sea. In a semi-circle facing the water were two weather-beaten shacks. The cove was pretty and raw, a seemingly primitive and untamed place in spite of the two shacks. But the overall effect was neutral, neither inviting nor uninviting, with a shore that was more dirt than sand and stringy green weeds sprouting randomly. A wooden dock extended about thirty feet from the shore, and there was a ladder at the end of it which descended into water that was perfectly still and as blue as the cloudless sky. On the ladder rested a faded red towel, fluttering lightly in the breeze.

We walked to the shack on the left. Harry pushed open the front door to reveal a musty room with a bare bed frame and, against the wall, a stained mattress. There was a small window at eye level against one wall and a single fire-lit stove. It took me all of thirty seconds to see it. It seemed most suited for a monk, a place for prayer and seclusion, which might be just what I needed. But I played stoic and unimpressed.

"You call this a villa?" I said to Martin.

He smiled. "One man's castle... as you Americans say."

There was no running water, and the entire shack looked as if somebody had once considered living there, but thought better of it. Walking around, I listened as Martin and Harry talked. My Greek was better than they thought, and I understood most of what they were saying. I heard Harry ask if I could pay in dollars, and Martin replied that I could, though there was no way he could know that.

"Hundred dollars US, every month, in advance," Martin said when we got back outside.

In Greek, I asked Harry about who lived in the other shack, to check if Martin had been truthful about this neighbor of mine.

A woman, Harry told me. He thought she was from Ireland.

"For feck's sake, Harry, *I'm* from Ireland," Martin said. "She's from *Australia*." Harry merely shrugged, one foreign country being the same as any other to him.

I walked out on the loose planks of the dock and fingered the red towel. A distant tanker glided by on the horizon, barely visible in the midday haze. I looked down past my feet at my reflection in the blue-green water beneath the dock and for a moment didn't know it was me. My black hair was long and wild. Around my blue eyes, my skin had already turned a few shades darker. My hand ran up to my chin and lingered on the hardened stubble, not something I was used to. It ushered me back to smoother-cheeked days, and in a symptom of longing or arrested development, I strolled through the museum of my youth, gazing at the exhibit of an eager and mystified boy, barely recognizable as me...

Standing on a plush, thickly shagged rug, a gray mass of bowed noodles. I curl my feet and catch the strands in the folds of my larger toes. A stale odor rises. The room is hot and little half-moons of fog form on the window panes. The bedroom of Mary Calhoun. Faded pink walls, desk, chair, bed, a winking teddy bear called Wayne, schoolbooks, tennis racket. Our clothes are in a pile between us. We have undressed ourselves, removing one article at a time, looking, revealing, then continuing in silence. I'm in white boxer shorts. Mary wears a thin white bra and sky-blue panties.

Mary's skin is a shade darker, her stomach flatter, shoulders and hips wider than I'd imagined. She appears shy and bold at the same time, standing before me with her arms crossed at the wrists, the fingers of one hand drumming lightly against the elastic top of her panties. She blinks slowly and continually; her eyes alive with the fear and excitement that accompanies the knowledge that this is a beginning and ending, a pivotal shift of things from unknown to known.

Mary's parents have gone away for the night and left us with her older brother, Brendan, who was under orders not to leave, but, of course, has done so. Mary and I know well that he'll not return for some time and that when he does, he'll be drunk. He'd offered us a bribe before he left the house, two cans of Budweiser, so we won't tell her parents he'd gone out. Now the empty beer cans lie on the bed where we'd petted and kissed. Cars pass by on the road outside, their headlights spotting momentarily beneath the heavy white shades of her window. The radio is on – "Shakin' that thing, yeah, yeah, like a diamond ring…" *– but I stay focused on Mary's breathing, which has become audible even as it grows shallower and more throaty, in and out, in and out.*

Part of me wants to play this like in a movie I'd seen somewhere, throw Mary down with controlled aggression and have my way with her as the man who knows what he's doing and takes what he wants. Of course, I neither know nor can take, and so I wait. We wait, but I feel we're taking an appalling chance. What if her brother or parents return? What if a neighbor needs to borrow milk? What if suddenly one of us gets sick? What if this possibility never presents itself again? But there is another part of me that wants nothing more than to savor this singular moment, knowing this is a memory that will never fade.

I feel an emptying sensation, sweaty hands pressed against my boxers. While looking down at her – I hadn't realized how short she was in her bare feet, making her seem so much less substantial, more strikingly vulnerable – I see the tiny laugh line near her left eye, almost not there, a perfect imperfection. I reach out to touch it, to make sure it's real and my eyes grow moist. I don't blink, afraid the moistness will compress into tears.

"Shakin' that thing, yeah, yeah, hear a ding dong ring."

We met in the eighth grade, smiled shyly when we passed in the halls, but rarely spoke for two years. I liked her, of course. She was a girl who flew under the radar, unremarkable in the remarkably unsubtle world of junior high, and possessing the sort of quiet prettiness you didn't notice unless you took the time. Unlike many of my peers, I did.

By sophomore year, I've spent hours, days, staring at her from the desk behind her or across the lunch room, studying the tapered ankles crossed right over left, and burnished hair pulled back in a red band, and, when I am close, the tiny laugh line. We ride the bus home together and begin to talk. She laughs at my jokes, lame as they must be, and one day calls me to tell me that she's still laughing at something I said. During the phone call, I mention a movie we'd talked about, an act of brilliant foresight. We go together that weekend, and at Holy Spirit High School in Brookline, Massachusetts, in the 1970s, that makes us boyfriend and girlfriend.

Over the next few years, Mary grows softer, fuller, pressing into her athletic lankiness a curved sultriness. Her youthful, somewhat restrained prettiness develops into sophisticated beauty that far surpasses what could have been predicted. Had I not known her so well, she would have become for a guy like me – a thin, formless boy, careless student, average athlete – unknowable and unreachable, threatening as a pointed gun. But I got in early, knew her too well, and vaguely understood – as best as a self-absorbed seventeen year old boy can – how her blossoming in this way sometimes made her uncomfortable.

She wasn't too coy to avoid comment, however. She'd tell me that if she'd known she'd develop in quite this way, would look this surprisingly good, she would've waited for better options than me. My customary response was that I had an eye for talent, which is often as important as the talent itself. She never pushed it too far, though, because the truth of the matter was that Mary *believed that her budding comeliness and sexuality was a gift, not just for her, but 'us' – as if somehow, talking, kissing and petting our way through three years of Catholic high school, we'd mated for life.*

So how could I have known that even as she stood naked in front of me – that even as I stood on the threshold of something which God, luck, and Mary's inviolable decency had granted me – that a part of me would step outside myself? It seems impossible to this day to believe so, but it's true that on this most significant day of my teenage life, a shadow consciousness is manifest and looks upon Mary, her purity, her delicacy, her trust, as a thing to be had, to be possessed. That I find within me a smirking man who regards Mary, nervous and achingly vulnerable in her white bra and blue panties, with a cold, hard, joyless eye – the vision of the occupier. So even before we begin, even as I run a finger over the tiny, tiny laugh line and with a tear in my eye, a part of me is already moving beyond this moment, pushing through Mary, charging beyond our innocence and tenderness. We fall to the ground...

The gentle sea splashed against the dock as the wake from that far off ship arrived in the cove. See-through waves rose as they circled the pylons of the dock, briefly stirring up some dirt beneath, and then went away as fast as they had arrived.

I didn't want to live next to a single woman of any nationality – I was trying to get away from all of that – but the possibility of waking up in a secluded cove and swimming every day before work was irresistible. I could simply let the woman know I wasn't interested in anything more than considerate neighborliness – if it ever came to that. I walked back to the entrance where Martin and Harry waited and told them I'd take it and move in the next day, if that was all right. Harry said sure, as long as he got the deposit. We all shook hands and then walked back through the tunnel of trees to Ari, who started the car as soon as he saw us coming.

The car rattled and clanked its way up the path as the branches scraped one side and then the other. And then it was: *en-ah, thee-oh, tree-ah* as we made our way back.

The tiny widow seemed distressed when I told her I was leaving. She said she'd enjoyed having me, even if we rarely spoke, and then added, with a weak smile, that it had been a long time since she had a man staying in the house. The morning I left, she kissed me on both cheeks, said she hoped I would soon find a nice girl, and gave me a batch of sticky cookies.

Duffel bag in tow, I hiked down the dusty road until I arrived at the cove and then moved into the shack. I lifted the stained, grimy mattress to the bed frame and made up the room as best I could. As the shack was tiny and my belongings were few, it took very little time. Later that day, I bought some supplies in the village and put these in the dusty cupboard when I came home from work at the taverna.

For one solid week of coming and going I never once spotted my neighbor, and I began to wonder if I ever would. The only evidence of her existence – indeed, the only sign of life whatsoever – was the red towel resting on the ladder. It became my habit to swim in the clear, blue water of the cove before work, and I always checked the towel before I did so. Once or twice, it seemed wet beyond the usual morning dampness.

I'd been on the island about a month at this point. During that time, work at the taverna was uneventful and routine: the men came, argued, played games and left; the kids played soccer and helped with the nets; the wives and daughters ran the shops. I was lonely and bored, which I suspected one should be during a self-imposed exile. Most days, I found myself drinking warm beer in the door of the taverna for hours, fretful and discontent.

Then one night the taverna was unusually full. Somebody's relatives from another island were visiting. There were about twenty of them, fathers, sons, brothers, cousins, and a whole over-extended family. They got rowdy as the evening went on, screaming and laughing and drinking what they believed to be Jack Daniel's until well after midnight. I wasn't sure what time it was when I finally locked the door.

A full white moon glistened above and lit my way along the dusty road back to the cove. The walk was pleasant, and I took it leisurely, thoughtfully, kicking up rocks and staring at the sky, until I turned off the road into the unpaved path that led to the cove. Because of the trees, the path was darker than the road, and I kept my eyes on the light coming from within the tree-tunnel just ahead. When I got there, I cleared the branches away with my hand. Just before I broke through the opening, I heard a chopped laugh and a big splash. Then there was laughter again. I stopped and stood in the loose dirt of the tunnel. Still in the dark myself, I was able to see ahead where the moon lit up the cove like a spotlight.

There, a woman traveled through the sea at incredible speed – but without kicking or moving her arms. In fact, there was no motion at all and no sound or evidence of a motor or propeller or mechanical device – only a slight ripping sound. The woman's head, framed in shadows, was thrust forward and strands of shoulder length hair flew behind her as she moved through the sea like the cap of a small wave. As she approached, only her head and shoulders were visible; the rest of her body was beneath the surface but somehow suspended, as if she were surfing on her chest. She stopped at the ladder and sank softly into the water. Grabbing onto the second rung, she shook her head violently like a dog, spraying water everywhere. She laughed, and the ripping sound stopped as the wake behind her silently formed a widening V.

Thin, with long wiry muscles, she climbed the stairs looking at the sea behind her. Her smallish breasts bounced slightly and her stomach flattened and tightened as she rose. Then she stood naked on the dock and seemed, above all, triumphant, like a predator reigning over the cove.

Another sound began, different from the one before; it was a type of etching noise but with a high pitch. The woman turned to face the sound, her back to me now. I watched a single drop of water wind down her back, creating a glazed stream that disappeared into the crease of her loins. Taking two large steps, she hurled herself up into the moonlight, gently spreading her arms and legs, her reflection gliding over the mirror of the sea. Landing in the water, she went down and then emerged, flying once again.

She sped away from me, the back of her head getting smaller and darker. She went to the edge of the cove, to the start of the open sea, and then began a slow circle back, almost levitating on the water, and rocking ever so slightly. When the circle was completed, she came to rest near the ladder. A sigh escaped her lips as she rolled onto her back. And there she floated, nose pointing at the stars, tiny ripples lilting over her stomach…

I don't know how long I stayed in the tunnel and watched the woman floating. Eventually, she climbed the stairs and dried herself with the red towel. When she finished, she spoke to the water and, exposed and proud, walked back to her shack.

Then the cove was deserted, silent and calm. And now the bright, limpid moon dangled far away, over another portion of the Aegean Sea.

2

I n ancient Greece, vengeful gods quarreled repeatedly in a
tumultuous soap opera set in heaven, hell and on earth.
There were many of these immortals, all dead now, from
whom one could ask deliverance, and one of them, it's safe to
assume, would likely grant it. In time, those all-too-human
gods had been replaced, of course, by a singular, more remote
Being, who bestowed His amazing grace on any wretch who
asked. But even He, it appeared, was gone now. Like the
fish in the Aegean Sea, our gods were diminishing. I, myself,
didn't know if I believed in that one God anymore, didn't
know if He could offer, with a tender sigh, the grace I sought.
It might've made things easier if I did believe, but I was an
agnostic man of my age, occasionally prayerful, often doubt-
ful. As such, the only redemption for which I could maintain
hope was mine to find. And this, to a large extent, was the
reason why I'd ended up on the island.

So as I made my way to work in the morning, though
the thrilling and unsettling vision of the woman in the cove
lingered, I tried to dismiss it. It was a distraction. I told
myself it'd been merely an apparition, a trick of the stars and
moon on my tired eyes. I'd heard of strange occurrences on
Greek islands before – tidal peculiarities, bizarre sea-creatures,

mermaid sightings, among others – and told myself that it might've been nothing more than the effects of dehydration, loneliness, or a lack of sleep. Though I knew this wasn't true, I stumbled forward, a pilgrim with blinders on, doing his best to take notice of only the next step.

I opened the taverna at the usual time and sat behind the bar trying to think of anything but the events of the previous night. It wasn't long until Harry, the fisherman-realtor, arrived and told me he owed money to Mr. Giorgos. He handed me a soggy paper bag which contained a massive tangle of the thick white legs and bulbous bodies of eleven octopuses, freshly caught and pulverized. The bag was heavy and wet and felt as if it might rip at any moment. I held it out in front of me dumbly, having no idea what to do, and resisted the urge to go and wash the smell from my hands.

Harry saw my confusion and helped me out. He took a fishing line and tied one end of it to the outside corner of the taverna. Then he attached the other end of the line to a wooden pole he had stuck in the ground. The line hung overhead, diagonally across the entrance of the taverna. "Sunning the octopuses", he explained in Greek as he methodically attached the eleven octopuses to the line with fishing hooks. They hung like giant white spiders, oozing a bluish, milky substance to the ground. Harry told me the octopuses should more than pay for his tab. I nodded, though I wasn't aware that Harry even had a tab, and went to wash my hands as soon as he left.

As the day progressed, women started coming to the door of the taverna for the first time since I'd been there. They asked for *octopothia* and handed over some money, usually 500 drachmas each. I'd sold all but three of the smaller octopus when Martin limped in on his black high-top sneakers.

"Who paid his tab?" he asked.

"Harry said he owed Mr. Giorgos some money. You know anything about that? Would it be written somewhere?"

"Giorgos' head. But you don't want to be goin' there, believe me, frightenin' place that. How much you chargin'?"

"Whatever they give me. 500 hundred drachmas on average."

"Shame on you, stealin' from these poor women like that. You *must* be CIA, fundin' somethin' covert somewhere."

"Maybe it's that I haven't gotten much direction from either of my bosses of which you are one."

"I like my employees to be self-motivated –"

"That's why I charged 500 –"

"– But not outright crooks. Take 100 drachmas for the octopus that remain, no more, then tell Harry his tab is paid." He sipped his beer thoughtfully. "*500* drachmas? Like exportin' food durin' the Famine." He finished his beer in three more gulps. "Seen your neighbor?" he asked.

I took a moment before answering, maybe too long. "Not yet."

"Sure?'

"I'd know, wouldn't I?"

I rose to stop Martin from staring at me.

"Beer me," Martin called.

I returned with two beers and placed one in front of Martin.

"Be needin' beer right now," he said, "for its' medicinal purposes. Beer is a diuretic, you know, urine and bowel provocateur, and presently I'm impenetrably constipated. Know what that means?"

"You can't go to the bathroom."

"Election time."

I laughed. "Elections make you constipated?"

"Or my constipation causes elections. Always presumed the former." He took a few drachma bills out of his pocket and flipped through them. "Isn't that a pretty site?" he said, handing one to me.

Drawn on the bill was a painfully thin man with his pants around his ankles, standing behind a large fish. The fish had a pained 'O' expression on his face, and the man had his arms raised in triumph.

"Ever met anyone whose beliefs are so far left, he ends up on the right, or vice versa?" Martin asked.

"I don't think so."

"Have now." He tossed the bill on the table and pointed to it. "Know who this is?"

When I shook my head, Martin pointed at a quick-eyed man sitting across the taverna. One of a few men who'd entered the taverna while we were talking, this man was no more than forty, quite young by island standards. The man spotted us looking at him and winked. Without any hurry, he rose from his chair and walked over. He was short, appeared to be underweight and was by far the best dressed man on the island, wearing clean Timberland shoes, khaki pants and a maroon Polo shirt.

"I've been away, but I've heard about you," he said. "My name is Kostas Giannopoulos." He spoke with a proper British accent and had a smooth dark face with a bulbous nose. "I am the one they say is –" he waved his hand dismissively, "the fish fucker and other unpleasant things."

"Kostas is runnin' for mayor," Martin chimed. "His father was a famous mayor, though fame on the island means nothin'. We're all famous here. But Kostas wants to be followin' in his father's large footsteps, only with better shirts."

"My father could have saved the island," Giannopoulos said, ignoring Martin. "Now it is my responsibility."

"Your accent is English," I said.

"I went to university in London." His manner was as loose as his speech was formal.

"So this is you?" I pointed at the drawing. There was indeed a slight likeness, more in the proportions than anything else.

"Not a good picture, I don't think, but it is me." He turned to Martin. "Have you ever heard of anyone fucking a *fish*?"

"Sea mammals mostly," Martin said, "backbone's helpful."

Kostas ignored this and continued talking. "These are proud men in this taverna, but there are too few of us and too many of the others. Papakakis is a greedy bastard. He wants to change the island, end the Marine Reserve, which limits pesticide use and certain types of fishing and keeps the island like it is. Like it always has been. But Papakakis has rich friends and, if he wins, will soon be rich himself. We can never return to the old ways if we get rid of the Reserve. Never. It is something that must be considered very carefully, very slowly. Not because a few stupid men want to get rich. You have seen the other taverna, the green one?"

"Of course."

"That's Papakakis' taverna. He owns it. He has connections and encourages his men to take more fish, use bigger and bigger nets, even against the law. Because once he kills all the fish, there will be nothing left to preserve and he will have won by default. Then we will have to bring in tourists, build hotels and restaurants, and be like every other island. But not every island has to be like that. Can there not be room for an island like this one? That is why you are here, no? To help us. You want something here. You are CIA, yes?"

It was near ten when I closed up, after Martin, himself, bought the remaining three small octopuses. Before heading to the cove, I decided to take a look at the other taverna

– Papakakis' green taverna. I lingered outside the door, peering into the dim light but standing in the dark, where they couldn't see me. There were still some men there, and these men mirrored the men in our own taverna. They were wearing the same clothes, drinking the same drinks, and playing the same games.

I recalled that Winston Churchill had once said that if you put three Greeks on an island, you'd end up with two Prime Ministers and a leader of the opposition. The fact that these two tavernas and nearly identical men had separated themselves into rivals attested to the truth of that aphorism. But here was the thing: these men *had* to live together. Unlike me – and with few exceptions like Mr. Giorgos – they had nowhere else to go. Saints and sinners shackled together, they were wholly dependent on one another, and the only grace they would ever receive was that which they bestowed upon themselves. For them, this island was the last – and only – place on earth.

One of the enemy fishermen shuffled out the door. I turned and looked away as he came out and then watched him shuffle along, head bowed, exhausted, shoes scuffing the ground as he disappeared into the village.

I sat down on an empty stoop and gazed along the jetty that curled out into the sea, a protective hook of giant rocks surrounding the pool of oily water in the harbor. By now the rest of the men had left the green taverna and the village was asleep, the doors and windows closed, the lights turned off. They went to bed early here; there was very little to do. There were no theaters, nightclubs or restaurants. Beside the two tavernas, the only other social life was what I was doing now, sitting, staring and thinking, which wasn't social at all.

I gazed at the tiny houses, snug on the hill behind me, and lost myself in the boy I'd been...

Lying together on the shag rug, my left leg riding across Mary's left thigh. We kiss, tongues gently invading, then pull away. I stroke her stomach, slick with sweat, and run my fingers through her tangled hair. No longer innocents, the act is done, but we're still filled with grace. Of this we are certain, having had it drilled into us for all our school years: that God's love is infinite and merciful, and though fallen, we are redeemed. There is a great and glorious plan – Thy will be done *– and we have a place and purpose in it.*

God's plan for today is this:

Condensation dripping through arcs of fog on the window sill. The thick shag carpet scratching my back and arms. Warm air from the heavy metal radiator. An upbeat song: "Hey ho, what's to know? Ho, hey, my baby say…" *Two empty beer cans on the bed. A horn in the street outside. The teddy bear, winking Wayne, against the wall. Her brother drunk somewhere. The Franciscan Sisters asleep in the convent. ("You're being saved for something special," they tell us, and heads bowed, we believe them.) Mary and I, saved, blessed, fallen, redeemed, at the center of it all. The snow lightly falling. I roll toward Mary and tell her I love her, because I do, I really do. I'm crying and no longer fighting it, no longer embarrassed by it, because it's done, because everything I will ever need is warm beside me right now.*

The smirking man, the shadow consciousness within me, despises this pathetic boy on the floor, his tears, his weakness, his vulnerability. He finds him naïve, immature, despicable. The only way to deliver myself is to reject all of this, reject Mary. He offers excitement, adventure, invulnerability, and Mary, because we did this, because we are so much alike, because we are in love, no longer offers any of this. Like the devil in the desert, the smirking man offers limitless, ecstatic possibilities. If I merely claim it, and reject the childlike Eden I have stumbled upon here. With Mary, the possibilities are already diminishing, he tells me. The act is done. I've learned something, thank God, I've grown up and I don't need to be a damn fool. Mary can offer only more of the same, nothing more than what I have right now – but with diminishing returns in a measured and casual castration, when the whole, wider world would've awaited, mine for the taking.

"Hey, ho, what's to know? Ho, hey, in every way."

The rush of time stops, the whir of the present moment – the endless shift of future into past – somehow ceases, and there, in this garden of plush, I run my little finger over Mary's tiny, tiny laugh line. She closes her eyes as I do so and it provokes a flood of warmth and pity. In that timeless, indefinable moment, I almost pull back from the man I would become, almost grant to Mary the love and vulnerability which she so willingly grants to me. Almost... but I pull my finger back from her face and in a blink, the decision is made. The smirking man becomes me, a boy-man incapable of gratitude, devoid of tenderness, a creature of scorn and greed and possession...

A sharp metallic sound rang out among the fishing boats, bringing me back to the island night, the graying harbor, the glowing houses. At first, it seemed to be no more than a rustling of the lines or a loose sail, but there was no breeze for that to happen, the crosswind of the late afternoon having long since departed. The harbor wasn't large, no more than three hundred yards across, and I scanned the fishing boats slowly, looking at half a dozen from bow to stern before I saw it – a phantom figure, half bent over in one of the boats to my left. It was a peculiar sight: a furtive, darkened figure against the peaceful, vacant backdrop of sea and sky. I moved closer, skimming the buildings as I skirted down the dusty road. I couldn't quite make out the phantom, but it appeared to be a woman or a young boy. The arms and legs were thin, the hair maybe shoulder length.

On the deck of each boat, the nets were clumped into two or three piles. And now, between the arms of what appeared to be large garden sheers, the phantom lifted the lines of netting on one of the boats and tried to cut through. But too many lines had been taken between the jaws of the clippers. The phantom knocked out a few lines and easily snipped the rest, which fell in uneven strings back to the deck.

Caught up in the stealth, I moved closer, and my right foot kicked a rock that scraped across the road. I froze. But the phantom, head bowed, was just then squeezing the clippers, which resounded with an echoing snap. While this was clearly an act of treachery, I felt it wasn't my place to intervene. I was a stranger here, a foreigner, and didn't want to intrude where I didn't belong.

The phantom was, of course, the woman I'd seen in the cove that night, gliding across the water.

I retreated back into the safety of a doorway and watched as she made her way through three more boats, meticulously cutting the nets on each and every one. When the destruction was complete and the final net lay severed on the deck of the last boat, she scampered away, up the dusty road and out of the village.

From a safe distance, I followed. I lost her once or twice around the corners but wasn't worried. I knew where she was going. Eventually, she turned off the road and went down the path, and I trailed her until she made her way through the tunnel of trees. When I arrived at the tunnel, I stopped and peered at the cove. In her shack, a candle flickered and then was gone. She was inside and safe.

My unmet neighbor.

3

The fishermen were livid.

They were waiting in an angry mob outside the taverna when I arrived around noon. It was the earliest they'd ever been there. Sweating, swearing and impatient, they filed past me as soon as I opened the door. I waited outside, looked across at the other side of the harbor and saw for the first time wives and daughters working in the fishing boats, diligently mending the nets. Bowed and silent in their dark skirts and blouses, they resembled nuns at prayer. Now and then, one of them would lift her head and wipe her brow with the hem of her skirt or take a drink of water. They took these actions quickly, furtively, as if there was a foreman standing over them, ready to dock their wages.

Inside the taverna, the men drank Greek coffee and ouzo and talked of defending themselves against Papakakis and his supporters. Through the next several minutes, I learned that the men from the two respective tavernas docked their boats on opposite ends of the harbor – and it was only the nets from Papakakis' side that had been cut. Papakakis was naturally blaming the fishermen from our taverna for the events of the night before and, with his men, plotting revenge.

I said nothing. It was not my island, I thought, and what went on between two groups of fishermen and a woman I'd never met was none of my concern. It wasn't just indifference, or even the vague pretensions of the disconnected pilgrim I intended to be, that kept me from speaking up, but something more. I didn't trust myself. Though I still believed (or thought I did) in the higher ideals I'd been taught as a child – compassion, courage, a sense of justice, the acknowledgement of beauty in living things – I no longer trusted in my ability to witness them or bring them about. I was numb, willfully distanced, and watched the fishermen as if actors on a stage.

At last, Giannopoulos arrived, dressed impeccably in a white button down shirt and blue pants. He surveyed the taverna carefully, saying nothing, eyeing every man.

"Papakakis better not do anything!" Harry screamed, his face turning a burnished brown color. "No one here cut those nets, you know that."

"We didn't do it, but I'm glad it happened." Ari said, banging his single arm on the table. "They deserved it."

Others joined in, pounding, screaming, alternatively attacking Papakakis and defending their innocence. They all kept an eye on Giannopoulos, however, as it seemed only he could give the final signal. After some time, he sighed and rose. He spoke softly, so the men couldn't talk and hear him at the same time. He advised the men to calm down, nothing had happened yet. To emphasize the point, he took a long, slow drink of ouzo. When he finished, he carefully placed the drink on the table and said he was going to talk to Papakakis. Then, almost leisurely, he walked out the front door.

Martin came in not long after. I brought him a beer and told him what happened. He mentioned that something like this had happened before: fishermen from Skopiathos, the nearest inhabited island, had come here and released a number of boats into the open sea. Fortunately, the men from our island caught the Skopiathians in time, before they could get to the last few boats, and were able to use these remaining boats to retrieve all the others. The Skopiathians claimed they were upset because of an invasion of their fishing waters. It could have been war, Martin went on, except that further trouble was averted when an inter-island marriage had brought the two places together. The men ironed out their differences over countless bottles of wine at the *glendi* that followed the wedding. But that was more than a decade ago, and there had been no trouble since then.

An hour or so later, when Giannopoulos returned, he gathered the men around him and told them that Papakakis had insisted he would do nothing to their nets or boats. The damage to the nets was not that bad, and Papakakis was willing to give them another chance.

"I made an agreement with Papakakis," Giannopoulos said, "The boats are not to be touched. Before, during, or after the election. For any reason."

Giannopoulos stared at each man, squarely, somberly, as he silently worked his way around the room. He said if both sides got into a battle, attacking each other's boats and nets, then they could forget about the Reserve, no matter who won the election. Once the boats and nets are destroyed, then Papakakis will have won, because all of them would have to find something else to do – the old way of life would be over. The *only* reason Papakakis agreed to a deal, Giannopoulos continued, is that he doesn't want anybody looking too closely at what's going on here, finding out about the illegal nets that his men are using.

"That would be a good thing," an elderly fisherman pointed out. "If they find out about the illegal nets, they might stop them."

"But once the boats and nets are destroyed, it will be too late," Giannopoulos countered.

"We barely have enough to eat as it is," Ari said. "How are we supposed to get through these days?"

The fishermen started rehashing their primary grievance against the other side: that Papakakis had already overfished the sea with those nets, and that the lifestyle they had lived and loved, subsistence fishing, was over. Giannopoulos clasped his hands behind his head and rocked back in his chair, letting them vent. It was as if he knew something like this would happen and had been preparing for it. He closed and opened his eyes sluggishly, as if awakening from a coma, and glanced around the room.

"Listen," he said, "here's what I'll do. I'll open up the fund once again and you can each get money, as much as you need."

Martin told me about this fund, which I'd not heard of until this moment. "Call it insurance," he said. "Men used to put in money for the ole' rainy day. Nothin' has been donated for a number of years as far as I know. All started by your man, Giannopoulos' father, when he was mayor."

At this time, a large man with a bright red beard called Yannis the Red rose from his chair. I recognized him as the man who had gotten drunk with Mr. Giorgos when I first started working on the island. He was easily the tallest fisherman and extraordinarily slow in his movements, as if he had to give each muscle twitch some thought. One of his hands massaged his beard as he spoke, and the other rested on the head of the scraggly dog by his side.

"Listen," he said, "we must hold out until the election, that is all we can do. I will learn to eat like Liza does, only scraps and leftovers." Liza was, of course, the dog by his side. A mid-size mutt with prominent Setter and Collie strains, she was one of those kindly, arthritic dogs, too tired and gentle to scratch a flea off her back. She gently licked Yannis the Red's hand as he spoke.

"Seen Liza before?" Martin asked me. "Preggers, due any day, and Yannis has been bringin' her with him everywhere so he'll know when the puppies are born. That way he can get rid of them. Too many dogs on this damn island as it is, and he doesn't want to add to the problem. Takes care of Liza as well as any man, but can't care for the pups."

I looked at Yannis and couldn't imagine him, no matter how hardened a man, strangling or clubbing Liza's puppies.

In the meantime, Giannopoulos had organized a backgammon tournament, promising the winner free drinks for a week. Around dinner, Martin brought in the three octopuses he'd bought the night before, and Yannis the Red made a small fire outside the taverna to cook them. The men drank, shared the octopus and played backgammon well into the night, as they had always done.

I left for the cove directly. The fire I'd seen on the mountain my very first night had somehow reignited. As I walked back to the cove, I glanced once over my shoulder at the orange flames bouncing in the night air. There was a time when I would have moved toward the flames with the purpose and anticipation that perhaps only a former firefighter understands. But those days were over, and I didn't allow myself another look before I ducked into the tunnel of trees that guarded the cove. Hidden by darkness, I stopped and spied inside.

My neighbor was there. Again she was soaring through the sea like the apparition I'd seen the first time. Only now she had one arm out and forward, and this arm seemed to pull her whole body. She was traveling at such speed that she had to twist her head away to keep the spray from splashing onto her face.

Into a slow curve she went and then started making her way back to the dock. Her eyes were raised as if she was navigating by the stars. Now, it was as if she started rocking on her waist, her head rising and falling, until her mouth opened, her eyes closed, and the cove went silent. Her forward motion stopped right next to the dock. She rested on her back for some time, then turned and stroked once toward the ladder. She climbed the steps, her breasts bouncing slightly against her chest, the water cascading down.

Despite myself, I again studied her naked body, a lithe, slender form of subtle arcs, leanly muscular. I tried to look away, to stay straight on the path of my pilgrimage, but the draw of this wet woman in the pale moonlight proved irresistible. She stood on the dock with her legs slightly spread, drying her face with the red towel. As I watched her, I felt for the first time in many months an inkling of desire, the abrupt visceral pull of wonder and lust, which I tried to ignore.

Suddenly, from behind her, a dolphin – recognizable by the smiling snout and dorsal fin – a dolphin bounded from the sea and flew into the air. She playfully flicked the towel in its direction as it crashed back to earth. Then she waited, towel cocked. The dolphin leapt on the other side of the dock, and she ran, laughing, to hit it. Missing widely, she replaced the towel on the stairs and said something I couldn't understand.

On the edge of the dock, she got down on all fours and dipped her head down until it was just above the surface of the water, which resembled a tabletop of black glass. She pursed her lips and produced a shrill whistle. Three feet away, the dolphin slipped its head above the surface. Silently it approached her. She lay on the dock now and opened her arms. The dolphin entered her embrace, placing its gentle, smiling snout on her shoulder. She hugged the dolphin tightly and placed big, sloppy kisses on its head and neck.

The dolphin pulled away, slightly opened its mouth and extended a thick, white tongue. She smiled, tapped it on the head and started to pet the tongue. The dolphin seemed to enjoy this, but after a short while the women playfully pushed it away. Then she got up and sauntered back to her shack, naked and proud, a startling, striding creature. I stared as she strode away: the crossing flow of her loins, the steady, rhythmic tense and release of her thighs and calves, her toes curling into the loose brown dirt.

A light went on in her shack and disappeared.

I broke through the tunnel and walked across the cove thinking: a dolphin and a strange woman frolicking together here, in this strange corner of the Aegean Sea. I didn't try to comprehend or interpret what I'd just seen. There seemed no reason to do so. A dolphin, was all I thought.

Cast across the sea by a dolphin.

4

In the morning, I headed to the village accompanied by the whine of a propeller overhead. A manila-colored seaplane was flying lazy parabolas over the mountain, occasionally slowing to expel an underbelly of water on the persistent fire. It must've been a small fire by now because, by the time I reached the village, the plane was leaving, and only few weak strands of smoke remained.

Most of the fishing boats had been repaired and had already departed. The village was nearly deserted, except for a single man with a bucket in his hand, standing on the platform that divided the harbor. As I got closer, I recognized the large red beard of Yannis the Red. He reached into the bucket and with his slow deliberate movements started throwing small, squirming objects into the sea.

It wasn't until I saw Martin sprinting across the dusty road, favoring his left leg, that I realized what those irregular objects were – Liza's puppies. I ran for the platform myself, hoping I might be able to convince Yannis to give me one. But before I got to him, Yannis dumped the bucket over the water, and a last ball of fur tumbled out. It yelped and splashed in the water just as Martin arrived.

Martin stood next to Yannis, peering intently into the water. From my vantage point, I could see a single solitary puppy struggling on the surface, the others having never re-emerged. The next instant, this last puppy went under, and Martin himself leapt into the water after it. For a few seconds, I could see nothing but a dark swirl where Martin had gone in. Then he emerged with the puppy scooped up in his arms. He held it out over the water and carefully made his way back to the platform.

By this time, I'd reached the platform and bent down, so Martin could hand me the puppy while he climbed up. The puppy was a tiny shivering sponge of fur and bones, crying in breathless, barely audible squawks. I held the puppy in two cupped hands, afraid that its soaked, tiny body would crumble if not fully supported. It rested its head, no bigger than my ear, against my fingers as its bony chest heaved in and out. I dried its face with my shirt and puffed warm breaths on its body.

When Martin climbed out of the water, I placed the puppy in his hands. After a quick look at Yannis, who merely shook his head in exasperation, Martin kissed the puppy's face and started back across the dusty road. I followed him.

"Don't know what came over me," Martin said as he made his way toward the village. "Just when you come into this feckin' world." He paused to catch his breath. "Couldn't let him drown, could I?" He limped up a pathway, passing chicken coops and drying laundry, and was gone.

I went directly to the taverna and started cleaning up. Martin had surprised me. It wasn't what he did exactly – diving into oily water to save the final puppy – but the way he did it. There was a sobriety to his actions. He'd been decisive, committed, intense – traits which I hadn't observed in him before.

I hadn't quite finished sweeping the floor when Ari came in. "We must talk," he said, pulling me with his single arm toward a table.

He sat on the next chair and leaned in until he was three inches away. He smelled strongly of old fish, and from this intimate distance his face reminded me of the bark of an olive tree. This was the first time a fisherman had sought me out, and I was curious about what he might have to say.

"I don't know why you are here, but I have ideas." He spoke the Greek slowly, making sure I'd understand every word. "The election is coming up and you are here to help."

"No. I'm not –" The last thing I wanted to discuss was island politics, or any politics for that matter.

"– No, no, I know. It is okay. Say nothing. Maybe you Americans need a secret base on the island, or maybe you want to re-fuel your submarines. You don't want a crowded, busy island. You want it like it is, so you can use it without the Russians or anybody knowing. If Giannopoulos wins, we can help you. We won't be puppets, but we will help. I will help."

He sniffed twice and rubbed his nose before continuing. "Papakakis has connections in Athens. People with money. People in politics. They are buying up land on the island. Cheap land. They have plans to bring on tourists, boats, hotels, you name it. Like every island in the Aegean. Like Skopiathos over there. Turn the whole place into rich men and poor men. Winners and losers.

"Right now, we are all the same here. I can't sell my fish for more than women can pay. They can't pay more than fishermen like me make. It goes round and round. The tavernas sell to us; we sell to the tavernas. It makes sense. There is balance. I have seen what happens when the new ways come. Fishermen become waiters, wives become cleaning ladies. One man gets rich while ten others work for him. Look, I am a simple man; I cannot read or write. I have been to Athens only once, when they cut off my arm because of the infection. But I like the way we used to live, before the illegal nets and all that. Life was good here."

He looked down at the floor and started making small circles with his feet.

"Not an important island, I know," he went on. "Not so pretty, not many fish left, but I live here and my wife lives here and others can live here as well. But if Papakakis wins, it will be the end of the Reserve. The truth is, what is being preserved here is not the fish. It is us. With those illegal nets, he is trying to catch all the fish, so there will be nothing left."

"Look, you need to know, I'm not a CIA agent. I work here at the taverna. That's all."

"It is okay. You are good, very good. You are quiet, you listen to everything, say nothing. That is very good, good training. It is okay, when you want to talk, we can talk. You help us and we will help you"

That was my first extended conversation with a fisherman.

The numerous cousins of Harry – all of them with midnight black, horseshoe-shaped mustaches curling around their mouths – had come in from Thessalonica that day for a child's baptism. They spent half the day and all the night drinking wine and ouzo at the taverna and steadfastly refused to leave. They were an important voting bloc, I understood, and Giannopoulos was buying all the drinks. It was quite late by the time they left, and I hurriedly cleaned up the place in order to return to the cove.

The first thing I saw as I started walking down the dusty road was the lurch of a mast. It was an unnatural movement in the quiet harbor, one that made me pause. I leaned in against the dark side of a building and saw the phantom again – my cunning, enigmatic neighbor – in the hull of a boat. Against the black surface of the sea, she was no more than a silhouette. She poured something from a plastic bottle and then bent down. I heard a *whoosh*, and she stepped quickly to the side as the bottom of the boat caught fire. It was a dark night, and the bright flame lit up the harbor like a spotlight.

Flames began to grow behind her as she leapt off that boat directly onto another. She repeated the same actions, and the second boat caught fire. I debated approaching the woman – I knew her actions would put an end to the handshake deal between Giannopoulos and Papakakis – when I heard a shout to my left. A fisherman had seen the flames and was running toward the boats.

The woman deftly slipped away, staying low and hiding behind other boats until she reached the dusty road. She looked back at the burning boats and then sprinted in my direction. The fisherman hadn't seen her; he was too busy charging toward the boats and yelling for help. The woman moved up the road and almost jumped when she spotted me in the darkness of the building. She hesitated for just an instant, astonished, before dashing up and away into the small streets of the village.

I waited against the building for some time, as more villagers came to the harbor. I suspected they'd have no difficulty putting out the contained fires with water, but I stayed and watched just in case. It didn't take long. When the fires were almost out, but before anyone had seen me and further suspected I was CIA, I started down the dusty road.

When I broke through the tunnel of trees to the cove, there was, for the first time, a light on in the other shack. The woman was leaning against the side of the open doorway. She waved me over and then disappeared inside. I momentarily considered ignoring her and acting as if I'd never seen her – now or in the harbor earlier. The damage she was doing to the nets and boats were not anything I wanted to know about, or be involved in. In addition, I wanted to keep as much physical distance between us as possible, having seen her naked in the cove those two times and felt the old stirrings. But I was weak and couldn't help but be curious. I rationalized that, sooner or later, we would have to talk and, since I'd probably have trouble sleeping this night anyway, I walked right into her shack.

Her place was a single room similar to mine – bed, stove, single window – except that it also had a small wooden desk, almost child-size.

"They're trying to destroy the Reserve with illegal nets," she said. She was sitting on the bed beside a strange and striking red and blue piece of corral.

Her voice, though of the scratchy variety, was quite soft, and I found myself leaning forward to hear. Proximity transformed her. No longer was she the phantom in the fishing boats or the creature upon the sea. The distance had hardened her features and now, close up, her face was rounder, gentler. She had dark sunken eyes and high but unpronounced cheekbones. She was a sturdy girl, haphazardly seductive in her faded, cut-off jeans and green tee shirt. The clothes draped unnaturally on her shoulders and hips. She was taller than I imagined, and thinner too. But the curves were somehow muted, as if the margins had been taken in.

"Here." She handed me a chipped white mug full of a syrupy brown liquid with black granules floating in it. She seemed to be radiating something, whether it was a residual of the day's sun on her skin, good health or a sort of understated sexuality, I couldn't quite tell.

"Coffee?" I said, surprised.

"Don't people offer that to each other?"

"Before midnight, usually."

She shrugged, and I noticed, written in thick letters on a scrap of paper above her desk, the number '187'.

"When did you make it?" I lifted the mug, which itself was cold.

"Three days ago, maybe more."

"That's an awfully long time for coffee to be sitting around." I took a sip. It tasted as bad as it looked.

"I'm just trying to get rid of the illegal nets," she said as I drank. "Or, at least, get a few days break from the onslaught. These guys have been here for five thousand years, and for five thousand years they caught what they ate. But now, now they're taking everything. If this sort of fishing continues, there'll be nothing left. *Nothing.* And the whole world will have died."

"It's an island, not the *whole* world."

She stared hard at me, wondering if this was a challenge. I took a hard swallow of coffee and stared back.

"Are you going to tell anyone it was me?" She said eventually. I let her think about this for a few long seconds.

"You lucked out with the right neighbor," I said eventually. "My plan is to stay out of all the politics and, frankly, everything else on this island."

"Right. So are you done with your coffee?"

I wasn't, but she took the mug anyway. She tossed the remaining liquid out the door and then considered the mug for a moment, before placing it on the counter.

"I don't want you to get the wrong idea," she said. "I'm pretty much a swim and let swim type. Rather neutral as far as humans are concerned."

"Except for the nets."

"*Illegal* nets. But believe me, I try to keep my vandalism to a minimum. Do no harm and all that, you know, that's my motto…" She smiled, but I couldn't return it.

An awkward pause elapsed. Nothing was said and, as we stared past each other, the silence between us seemed to expand, relieved only by the scratching sound of crickets.

"Kerryn," she said eventually, extending a thin brown hand. I shook it, told her my name and took that as a signal to leave.

5

Two fishing boats remained in the harbor the next morning. Slowly, a thick rubber mallet arced up from the middle of one of the boats, lingered and then crashed down. A hollow, muted *thud*, like a stomped foot, echoed across the otherwise silent harbor. This was repeated two or three times. Just after, Martin himself raised his head from the boat and wiped his brow. It seemed strange to see Martin on a fishing boat, but it was stranger still to see him working.

"How's the puppy?" I asked as I approached.

"Home. Not up to travelin' yet."

I leaned over and peered inside the boat, which reeked of ash, fish and gasoline. The damage was more severe than I'd realized the night before. The fire had singed a good portion of the lower hull, and a small uneven hole of a few inches in diameter had burned through a thin section. Three inches of oily water had pooled into the bottom of the boat, causing Martin's black sneakers to suck and squish as he labored.

"This is one of Papakakis' men's boats, isn't it?"

Martin looked up at me. "Giannopoulos' idea. Sent me out on a peacekeepin' mission to fix their boats."

I nodded and watched him. "So this how you support yourself?" I said after some time.

"This is how I support others. The way I support myself is with delusional thinkin' and alcohol." He put down his tools and sat at the edge of the boat, raising his dripping sneakers out of the oily broth in the bottom of boat. "This work is fairly new to me. I knew how to fix many things in Ireland, but not boats. This trade I picked up here. I've always been a decent handyman, which comes in handy."

It was still early, with the sun lingering at a sharp angle over the sea. I was in no hurry to open the taverna and sat down on the dock. "Is that what you did in Ireland? Handyman?"

He took his hat off and wiped sweat from his forehead. "Close enough. Lived on the borderlands between north and south, survivin' on dreams, ideals and foolishness with a bunch of dreamy dreamers, idealist idealists and foolish fools."

"Which of those were you?"

"All three. Everyone knew we'd all end up dead or in prison. What no one ever considered a possibility – as I'm sure ole Napoleon Bone didn't consider either – is exile to a tiny island."

He went back to work. As I watched him, I thought about how alike we might be, both of us serving self-imposed (or not) exiles on this island. We were kindred spirits, if forged of different material. I think he sensed as much, as well. You didn't just accidentally arrive on this 'God and beast forsaken island.' It was too far away, too poor, too obscure. No, you were either born here, like the fishermen, or arrived the way Martin and I had, as outcasts and emotional refugees.

"Doesn't look too good," I said, pointing my chin to the boat.

Martin leaned down, picked up the mallet and weighed it with his hand. "Two boats lit on fire, and comin' right after the nets were cut. Papakakis' men haven't put it together yet. They're thinkin' it's an accident or some election stunt, but not me. Giannopoulos is right. No one on his side would be messin' with the nets or the boats. Their own are too vulnerable. So if it wasn't a fisherman, it had to be someone else."

"I guess."

"But this isn't feckin' New York City, my friend. Not too many else's around. Know what I mean?" He squinted up at me from the boat, planted his sneakers in the oily pool of water in the hull, and went back to work.

Standing on the dock at the cove the next morning, I saw a million finger-sized fish in the unmoving green water beneath me. On command, they darted at odd angles forming 'Z' patterns in quick precise bursts. Timing their moves, I dove on top of them and chased them as they scattered. I followed them from beneath the water and shot out my hand to touch the stragglers. But it was no use, and after a few unsuccessful stabs, I climbed the ladder and dried my face with the red towel.

"I have coffee," Kerryn called from the doorway of her shack. She stood in cut-off blue jean shorts and a green bikini top, her arms the color of maple syrup.

"The same three day old coffee?"

"Of course not," she said. "It's four days old now."

I smiled – she had me there – then slowly walked over to her shack, letting the water on my body evaporate in the intensifying morning heat.

There was now a large pile of junk in the middle of the room: a pair of socks, a bra, a towel, two pencils, cups, plates, a brush and comb set, some random clothes, a book, and many more things I couldn't make out. On the paper above her desk, '187' had been crossed out; beneath it was written '127'. Kerryn handed me a nicked mug as I entered, filled with mud-like coffee.

I took a sip. "This coffee sucked yesterday, and is worse today."

"Want that mug?"

"Just the bad coffee will do, thanks."

"Take the mug. You can have it."

"If we're exchanging neighborly gifts –"

"It's not a gift." She said as she walked over to the other side of the room, "In fact, it's exactly the opposite." She took the paper from her desk, crossed out the number '127' and wrote '126' just below it. She crossed back to my side of the room, and I noticed a certain conservation of movement in her actions, a calm purposefulness. She leaned against the counter, poking a bare hipbone in my direction above the top of her shorts.

The front door had been left open, and a lazy, sultry breeze wafted in. I took in a vague aroma, a sort of warm bread and butter scent that emanated from Kerryn's body. As I stood next to her, the image of her on the dock kept entering my mind: the slight outward slope of her naked waist, the single drop of water disappearing into her loins. I spoke to purge the picture.

"What's with the numbers?"

"That's the number of my possessions. Do you know how many things you own?"

"A lot less than I used to. How do you count a pair of socks, for example? Is that one or two?"

"Two. Everything counts, every sock, pencil, picture, your bed, bed frame, radio, TV, soap, towels, toothbrush, clothes, everything."

"Not making things easy on yourself." I took a sip of the coffee, swallowing a few bitter grains.

"I don't think of getting rid of things as a burden, I think keeping them is. That's why that mug isn't really a gift."

"The coffee's no gift, that's for sure." She laughed at my modest joke. It seemed to be the uninhibited and infectious laugh of a woman who didn't take herself too seriously – though given the meticulous manner in which she counted her possessions, I wasn't too sure on that score.

"What're they saying about the burned boats?" she asked, looking away.

"Well, Martin practically said that he knew you did it."

"Right, he would know. I've tried to get rid of the nets before, and he knows that." She tugged on the strap of her top, letting it snap back. "I've written letters about it, made some phone calls. I came here to research dolphin behavior. There were five others with me at first, but they left about a year ago, and I stayed on. Anyway, I've written to environmental groups in Athens and everywhere else, and told them how important the Reserve is, and about all the fish and seals and dolphins that live here, and how the illegal nets threaten them."

"Any response?"

"When I got one, it was that they'd need evidence that someone was breaking the law. I don't know how I could gather evidence. Some pictures, I guess, but what would those do? Papakakis is a shrewd man and knows what he wants."

"To turn the island into a tourist destination."

"And destroy everything that makes this place so special. You know one thing special about this place? They made almost no garbage here. Ever. *None*. For five thousand years, they basically didn't produce waste. If they start developing, they'll have to bring in junk and packages and food and produce *garbage*. They'll need landfills to store it. Don't you think it's ironic that the less natural resources they have, the more waste they'll produce? I'm on *their* side. I am. I admire these people and want things to stay as they are."

"Shouldn't the people here decide what they want to do with their own island?"

"Somebody has to take a stand, somewhere."

I shrugged. I didn't bother to point out that Giannopoulos was doing just that, or that if anyone was going to take a stand here, it should probably be a local like him – not an outsider or a foreigner. I said nothing, however, not wanting to involve myself in such a discussion. I finished my coffee in a single unpleasant gulp.

She arched back on the counter, stretching her neck and lengthening her stomach. Then she rocked over forward and, with that certain economy of movement, touched her toes.

"There's going to be an eclipse tonight around midnight," she said to the floor. "Ever seen one?" She straightened up, flicked her black bangs off her forehead and turned to me.

Our eyes held for an instant – until I looked away, out the open door to the dock planks broiling helplessly in the sun. I told her I had to get to work and started to hand her the coffee mug. She grinned, raised her hands and backed away as if it was radioactive. I shrugged, kept the mug and walked out of her shack into the blinding light.

6

I stood in the door of the taverna watching the local kids play soccer and rolling a long blade of grass between my teeth. As far as I could tell, every boy on the island took part in this daily game. They played without strategy or order, three, four or five of them around the ball at one time, kicking simultaneously, their screams along with errant balls careening off the walls of the surrounding buildings.

In time, I saw Mr. Giorgos, owner itinerant, walking towards the taverna on the dusty road. He looked refreshed and re-energized from his trip to Italy. His hair sported a slick, sway back style (the one fashion on the island could best be called 'unwashed and unkempt chic'), and his face looked as polished as a Renaissance restoration project. Eschewing any greeting, he walked over to the card board box and counted the money inside. There wasn't much money there because, as instructed, I'd been regularly depositing the receipts with Savvas at the bank. Mr. Giorgos then took out his most recent bank statement from Savvas and added the amount in the bank to the cash in the card board box.

"I think you are not stealing from me," he said finally.

"Would I still be here if I was?"

He gave me a bonus, five thousand drachmas. I looked at the bill: Giannopoulos had a black rose between his teeth and was either running or dancing behind a mule, his eyes wild, his pants around his skinny ankles.

Mr. Giorgos then appraised the taverna and, apparently, found it satisfactory. When the fishermen started filing in, he swaggered around, greeting them. He was something of a celebrity, of course, being the taverna owner and world traveler, and he wasted no time describing his adventures in Italy. He'd just started describing how he was pick-pocketed in Milan when Martin walked in, wearing an impossibly hot army jacket. Mr. Giorgos kissed Martin on both cheeks and continued his story, describing how he'd leapt onto the back of the thief and bitten his neck like the head of an octopus. The thief fell to the ground stunned, and that's how Mr. Giorgos got his wallet back.

"Bet you didn't know that," Martin said to me as I handed him a beer. He had left his jacket on as he sat down, carefully stretching the side so it hung over the side of the chair. "How a fisherman paralyzes an octopus without a knife."

"Bites it?"

"Head to head, mouth to mollusk, teeth to brain." Large beads of sweat materialized on Martin's forehead. They raced down his nose and cheeks, leaving dirty streaking lines. Martin rubbed his scarred knee, then eyed the corners of the taverna in mock suspicion and flipped opened the flap of his jacket. There, tucked into the inside pocket, was a wide-eyed, red fuzz ball nursing on the nipple of a small bottle of milk.

"Named him Bobby," he said.

Mr. Giorgos interrupted us by putting a heavy arm around Martin and kissing him on the top of the head. The story of the retrieved wallet had concluded in an Italian hotel room, with Mr. Giorgos and a loose-limbed Venetian beauty performing impossible sexual contortions. I didn't know whether to believe it or not.

"He is the whole boss to you now," Mr. Giorgos said to me about Martin, who was petting Bobby's head with his calloused thumb. "I will leave again. Italy was so good, I want to see Spain. Madrid, Valencia, Majorca, I want to see it all. The spicy Spanish women, they dance to seduce the devil."

"Didn't you just get back?"

"Only to check-up on you. Now I will stay away longer, one month, maybe more. I am, how you say, tired of the taverna work. I have a little money and I am wanting to see the world. You keep doing exactly what you are doing." He scraped his feet across the floor. "Maybe you sweep once in a while. Any problems, you talk to Martin." He paused, then added, "You Americans, you are not small thieves, I think. Big thieves, yes, but not small thieves."

When I arrived at the cove after work and sat on the dock, there was a dull reddish glow on the opposite side of the mountain that could only have been another fire. A single manila seaplane flew in the opposite direction of the full moon and disappeared behind the mountain. The whine of the engine faded just after, and I was left to the sound of my own breath.

As I sat alone in this isolated, verdant enclosure of Aegean waters, in expectation of a rare and mysterious planetary alignment, something inside me came alive, an almost animate eagerness and attentiveness that transformed everything, even the cove itself. I pivoted slowly.

Surrounding me now in varying shades of gray were the bare mountain towering majestically with a fire sparkling red and yellow; a half circle of lush colorless pines, bushes and shrubs fencing the cove and forming, at the entrance, the black tunnel to another world; the wet expanse extending from the dock and stretching to the curved horizon. In the softness of the elapsed dusk with the low angle moonlight glancing in, the cove seemed the fountainhead of all the dark waters of the sea, nothing less than the sustaining and nourishing womb of all the earth's oceans.

Just as I was mesmerized by the hard beauty of the cove, I was startled by approaching footfalls on the dock. Kerryn was behind me. She took a running leap right next to my head and slipped into the sea. She circled beneath the water.

"Shouldn't be long now," she said, emerging at the stairs. She stepped onto the dock, clad in her blue jean shorts and a white tee-shirt tied in a knot below the ribs – clothes that I now noticed she seemed to wear unnaturally, like uncomfortable and inessential encumbrances or sackcloths. She dried her face with the red towel, then plopped down next to me.

We sat in silent anticipation. I tried to take it all in, the large white bottle cap of the moon in a sky that was forever racing outward and into nowhere. For several long minutes, I tried to imagine it all expanding, gobbling up space that, just a second before, didn't exist. The common feeling at times like this is one of insignificance, but that wasn't true for me. My feeling was more like reassurance that one day there might be enough room for all of us.

"Now," Kerryn said, breaking the silence and pointing.

At that moment, the white round edge of the moon was touched by the orange shadow of our own planet. The rest of the moon brightened and flared from beneath the edge of this coppery covering. Then as we stared in silence, the earth's shadow crept silently and steadily across the face of the moon. A murkiness began to occupy the night air, and suddenly a ripping sound began, faint and distant, but getting louder. I lowered my gaze and saw a fin spring from the end of the cove, cutting the surface of the water. A clicking sound started, resembling one of those whirling New Year's Eve toys.

"Of course," Kerryn said, "there's no way she'd miss this." She slid from the edge of the dock and under the water with barely a splash. Immediately she came up. "She turned around. I think you scared her away." She swam to the ladder. "Come in."

I thought about this for a moment, but not too long. There was something dangerous and magical about the arrival of a dolphin in the darkening night that, like the eclipse, was too alluring to resist. I removed my shoes and shirt and jumped in.

"Try not to be scared or nervous," Kerryn said. "Dolphins have an echo system, like ultra sound. They can actually sense out emotions, so remain calm. Don't worry."

We were treading water about ten feet from the dock. Kerryn slapped her hand on the surface, stopped and repeated. Then she produced the whistling sound I had heard a few nights earlier. The sound rang out across the sea, and the fin appeared from below, but with none of the advance warnings that had preceded it before, none of the ripping or clicking. As silently and suddenly as the first drop in a sun shower, the dolphin surfaced next to Kerryn.

Instinctively, I pulled back. The dolphin was much larger than I'd imagined, heavier and yet more sleek. It had a large, long gray body that was made for speed; a body that looked in motion even when it was stopped. Kerryn pivoted the dolphin, floating effortlessly in the water, so that it faced me.

The eyes were like that of a prodigious child – eager, vivid, intense – taking in everything. As I peered into the large black ovals I knew, if only for their quickness and clearness, that I was greeting a higher intelligence. If not for the perceptible gentleness, the dolphin could have appeared too smart, too powerful and for that reason come across as sinister. But a certain curiosity and playfulness came through. The dolphin was looking at me, seemingly amused, and I found myself being calmed.

Kerryn called me over. She shifted the hulking body of the dolphin in the water. Beneath the wide slit of the smiling mouth were rounded jowls as if the dolphin were chewing tobacco. With such jowls, which I'd never seen on a dolphin before, it looked like a politician, a back room wheeler-dealer.

"This is Yukon," Kerryn said. She spoke in a high pitch voice, laced with affection.

Yukon opened her mouth, and I found myself staring at the hundreds of small white teeth on the bottom of her jaw. Then Yukon stuck her great pale pink tongue out at me. I stuck out mine. Kerryn laughed and petted the dolphin's tongue.

"Try it," she said. "Go ahead."

I placed my hand between the teeth of the dolphin and pet the tongue. I wasn't nervous, and it was only after that I'd realized exactly what I'd done. The tongue was rough and firm, the texture of over-cooked chicken. The dolphin wagged her head as I took my hand out, dove under the water, and came up next to me, splashing water on my face.

"The great Yukon," Kerryn laughed.

It was as if time had stopped. I put my arm around the dolphin and held myself above the water. I couldn't prevent myself from laughing as well, imbued as I was with a light, sweet emotion. Touching its body – the first time I'd ever touched a wild animal in its natural environment – somehow empowered me. I felt released and unburdened.

Yukon ducked under my hand, swam ahead of me, made a sharp turn and came back. There was a white ball tethered to the bottom of the dock and floating in the water. I had never noticed it before, nor the wooden peach basket above it until now, when Yukon smacked the ball up and into the basket. A perfect shot.

"That's how I know if Yukon's been here when I'm away," Kerryn said. "The ball's in the basket. It's our signal."

Kerryn swam over and pulled the ball out of the basket. As she came back, Yukon burst out of the water and flew an aquiline path over Kerryn's head. Watching the dolphin pierce the air, I noticed the darkness that now blanketed the cove and cast my gaze back to the moon.

"There it is," I said, and the night deepened further as the entire face of the moon was covered by a perfectly sized penny of copper. All light was swallowed, and the night existed in the belly of darkness. Right next to me, I heard Yukon splash from the surface and gush water out of her blowhole. She squeaked and clicked as the water rained down on me. I twisted and reached out blindly to touch her, but she was gone. In the distance, I heard a screeched articulation of dolphin joy.

Seconds later, when a sliver of the moon had reappeared on the reverse side, Yukon flipped out of the water at the far end of the cove, going away with another screech.

"She's a sassy one," Kerryn said as we climbed back to the dock. "Sweet too. I think she likes you."

I stood behind Kerryn as the light of the moon slowly re-emerged, burgeoning in luster with each passing second. Speckles of salt on Kerryn's neck and shoulders glistened in the returning light. She turned toward me and her eyes, dark and deep, beamed as bright as the uncovered moon. Silence settled over the cove, and it was as if it had never happened, as if the dolphin had merely been part of a trance that included the darkening and brightening night.

7

The taverna was slow all day. Very few of the fishermen came in. I thought that maybe they were catching up on the fishing they'd missed, and the fish were at long last biting, or else they were just tired. Whatever it was, I was grateful for the respite and content to let the time slide by as slowly and benignly as a ship on the horizon, returning again to the museum of my past...

I pass all the requisite tests for the Boston Fire Department, and Mary goes on to a small Catholic college in Worcester. I've rejected the idea of college. I'm a mediocre student at best and can't find an academic subject that interests me. I'd also done some quick calculations. Firemen are relatively well paid and get lots of time off. With the odd jobs I could pick up on my free days, plus the extra four years of income versus expenses, it was really the only decision. Pack some cash away, make some shrewd investments (gold? real estate?), and I could be both working class hero and, in time, unassuming millionaire.

An added benefit is that becoming a fireman is a way to underscore the break with Mary, put a useful socio-demographic barrier between us. (At least for the time being, until my gold and real estate investments pay off.) There is some stilted talk between us about staying together – Worcester being only sixty minutes from Boston – but that ends with nonsensical blabber about my youth and freedom, and then, contradictorily, work and commitment. Mary is disbelieving, then outraged, then silent – and that's how she remains. Not that I'm too unhappy about it. Even if there are the subsequent long nights when I think about what could have been, these occur less and less frequently, until they are finally non-existent.

The firehouse is a frat house. No women are assigned to our station, and I am wanton, crude and, in the off hours, largely drunk. I use my minor celebrity as the man in uniform who saves babies, cats and old ladies to seduce the fawning and prey on the unsuspecting. The only thing I may not have – yet – is money, the sort of money some women want anyway, but I write those women off as benevolents (feeling benevolent as I do so), who would one day marry a sugar daddy and, in moments of nostalgic weakness ("oh, that brave fireman I once knew…"), provide for the upkeep of the station with overgenerous donations. Every woman has her place in my world as I stand outside the station on Washington Street with kind words and a just-here-to-help smile.

Four older guys in our station are married, and they make sure, as best they can, we train hard and show up sober to our shifts. The younger of us are mostly single; only one, my best friend, Steve Martinis, is married to the fab Francesca, as we call her. With impenetrable black eyes and sheer olive skin, street-smart and funny, in tight black jeans and tank tops, she hails from the Italian North End of Boston. None of us can figure out what she's doing with Steve, and most of us have a vague crush on her, although mine is full blown.

Francesca and I often talk. During long nights at the Coolidge Corner Grill, when Steve is playing darts or doing shots with the boys, I inevitably find my way over to her. We understand each other, are mutually attracted (I think), and after a few beers the words come easy. One time, I ask how Steve ended up with a girl like her, and she says without hesitation, "I couldn't imagine life without him." I don't believe her.

And on a very drunken night a few weeks later, "Did you ever think about you and me? Say, if we'd met first."

"Dangerous question," she says, then toasts me with her pint, knocking back a solid inch of beer. She leans in close; on her upper lip is a white layer of foam. Her breath is heavy, and I can smell a faint mixture of sweat and perfume coming from her neck and shoulders. Her face is next to mine now, and just as I think she is going to kiss me, she lifts the sleeve of my Boston Fire Department *tee shirt with two fingers and wipes the foam from her lip.*

The corner of her full mouth turns up in a slight smile. "Thought I was going to kiss you, didn't you?" It's not the first time she's done this. And if she leaned over and picked something up on the ground, raising her dewy eyes to me while exposing a generous gift of cleavage, it wouldn't have been the first time for that either.

I'm drunk. In an unsteady moment, I almost, almost wonder what I am doing. But these are days that I live without introspection. With the slimmest dint of self-examination, I might've comprehended the spite and ugliness in the cliché of your best friend's wife, might have realized how we were playing each other. But there is no thought as to 'why' or 'what for' anymore, no purpose or plan to these smirk-filled days beyond the next drink, the next conquest, and Francesca's tight black jeans.

Steve approaches. "You two are always together," he says guilelessly and gives Francesca an affectionate slap on her backside. I suppress a wince as her back straightens in response, and they kiss.

I glance around the bar and see another woman, short and bouncy, playing darts, bobbing to the music: 'Come to Poppa.

Come to Poppa, little Princess...' *Her disproportionately large chest stretches the 'e' and 'o' in the 'Red Sox', written across her shirt to comical proportions. We catch eyes and she seems just the sort to be enamored with a working class hero, drinker and charmer and an easy target for this evening. I smile shrewdly at Francesca then saunter over to the woman with a bold, welcoming smile.*

'Poppa's got the wisdom. Poppa's got the goods...'

"Run and play," Francesca calls behind me.

The short, buxom girl comes home with me. She is impressively uninhibited, surprisingly inventive, more than I could've hoped for. I send her off in the morning in my Boston Fire Department *tee shirt, then wait until Steve starts his early shift and call the fab Francesca to tell her all about it, beat by beat by beat.*

In the course of this and other days at the taverna, I often wondered what made me think I'd achieve any degree of success in this self-described pilgrimage to another land. I'd lived as a smirking man for so long, why did I suppose I could remake myself? It couldn't merely have been the result of my newfound self-awareness and introspection. That had only made me aware of what I'd done and purchased the ticket for my departure from Boston, but suggested no promise of reform.

Somehow, despite all I'd done and who I'd become, I still believed I could tap into an undiscovered recess of my soul (for lack of a better term) and find those things – compassion, courage, the acknowledgement of beauty – that had been cast aside. The only reason I could arrive at for the inextinguishable nature of that belief was that there had been people, Franciscan nuns telling me I was saved for something special, Mary loving me, firemen trusting me with their lives, who must've seen within me something worthwhile – perhaps the best definition of a friend.

Though I'd betrayed each of these people in great and small ways, I believed in them, in *their* faith in me. That, of course, gave me no claim on them, but, I reflected, it might indeed give them some claim on me – even if I was gone far away and they, my believers, were forever lost to me.

At the cove, Kerryn was standing on the second step of the ladder, petting Yukon, who floated listlessly below her. Yukon appeared different than before, zapped of energy and exhibiting none of her usual playfulness or exuberance. Kerryn, too, seemed tired and distracted as she palmed little scoops of water onto Yukon's back.

Kerryn hadn't heard me approach, and I hesitated before reaching the dock, taking in the taught, lean muscles in her shoulders, the galaxy of tiny, maple freckles across her back. I could feel my resistance further weakening. I'd been able to curtail most – certainly not all – of my thoughts of a sensual nature, it was true, but she was getting to me in small and indirect ways. The biggest, of course, was Yukon. When I'd touched Yukon, I'd felt relieved of everything I'd once done and been for the first time since I'd left Boston, existing momentarily as I imagined a Buddhist monk might in his unattached and enlightened void. And I longed to return.

I stepped onto the dock to greet them both. Kerryn turned around as soon as she heard me, and a delicate tear trickled down her cheek.

"Yukon's been hurt."

Kerryn re-positioned Yukon so I could get a better view. There were two large white streaks on her right side, just below the dorsal fin; each gash was eight or ten inches long, an inch or so deep. She was such a large creature, that I was stunned. Who or what could have done this? Yukon looked straight ahead as I inspected the wounds from the dock, eyes focused on something in the distance like an anesthetized patient. She was either too proud, too hurt or too angry to look my way.

"They could have come from anywhere," Kerryn said. "It doesn't look like another dolphin. They do rake each other once in a while, but... I don't know."

"Was it one of the nets?"

"The nets wouldn't scrape her like this, I don't think. Maybe. I don't know. If it was a net, she's lucky to be alive. If she gets caught in one of those, then..."

As we talked, Yukon drifted away from the dock. Kerryn dropped into the water once to rinse, then picked herself up on the stairs and wrapped her arms around me. I froze, held myself rigid against her body as she looked up, her dark eyes puffy red and her skin smelling of the sun and sea.

"When something like this happens, it makes me realize..."

She clenched the back of my shirt in her fists. Teardrops dripped down my chest.

For a few long moments, I didn't hug her back, until the fall of my arms became too awkward and I put them around her. We stood as still as stars in the sky, her heart thumping in my chest, my arms against the heated skin of her back. She pulled me tighter, her feverish body leaning into mine. I felt another inkling of desire and put her at arms length, my hands remaining on her shoulders.

"It's not the first time," she said. "It's happened before. It's a fact of nature. But every time I get more scared. It's just Yukon and me here, you know, and if anything..."

As she was about to break down, she pulled away and toughened herself almost instantly. I saw that she wasn't the sort of woman who would let herself weaken too much. Alone on the island, she'd not been able to rely on others for emotional support and didn't intend to start now.

"I think that Yukon's injury is a sign," she said. "A bad one."

The night was cloudy, and there was no moon and no breeze. Some brave stars peaked through the clouds and were rewarded by shining twice on the dual canvases of sky and sea. A lone cricket chirped in the distance, near the tunnel, as Yukon re-entered the cove, the telltale ripping sound of her dorsal fin heralding her return.

Kerryn immediately took off her shirt and shorts; there was no hesitation or shame in her actions. Like everything else I'd seen her do, there was a naturalness to it, an unimpeachable authenticity and certainty. She stood in front of me naked and must've known that this was something I wasn't accustomed to, especially as an American. Women rarely stripped in front of men in Boston unless they were getting into a shower, a bed or were being paid to do so. Since Kerryn appeared to lack any self-consciousness about her body, I tried to act as if I wasn't conscious of it either, staring into her dark eyes and letting myself only glance across her thin, brown legs in the course of looking down at Yukon.

She jumped in the water and swam toward Yukon. As I watched from the dock, I wondered how it all started. For Yukon wasn't in any way domesticated as far as I could tell. Yet, untamed, she swam here every day of her own volition. There was no real reward, no amount a food that could satisfy a dolphin's appetite, only Kerryn. They seemed equal, consenting partners in the most genuine way – friends for the sake of friendship.

As Kerryn tread water, she called back up to the dock. "The island is changing. Everything anyone would ever need is here right now, but greed is going to change all that." She slapped the top of the water with her hand and made a shrill whistle sound. "You coming?" she said.

I left my clothes in a pile on the dock and dove in. I surfaced next to Kerryn and instantly heard the ripping sound again. The dorsal fin approached from the corner of the cove, severing the water like the sharpest knife. Ten feet in front of us, it disappeared. Kerryn cried out. Instantly she was connected to the dolphin. They brushed by my legs lightly and then, in seconds, were at the far end of the cove. I watched as they played out there for a while, rolling, diving and twisting.

They returned at high speed. Kerryn stared at me, eyes wide and rapturous, as she came closer. Yukon deposited Kerryn about two feet away. She climbed the steps to the dock. I felt a strong current next to my waist and sensed a large presence. Then there was a rub against my back, a gentle hello. Next the dolphin glided by, barely touching, slipping and sliding by as if I were oiled.

My senses were amplified; I could feel the water slide between my calves, the pulse in my veins, a tightening in my eardrums and then, a sensation that I'd never felt before, an inner tremor or a gentle shaking from the inside out. The sensation ended as quickly as it started and just as I was getting used to it. It seemed like Yukon was teasing me, hinting the possibility of something I hadn't yet imagined. I searched across the glassy water looking for her, hoping for her return.

"That was good-bye," Kerryn said.

I climbed up the steps, and then we stood on the dock, inhaling the night air fresh off the sea and staring at the cove, now black and glassy, having erased all evidence of dolphin and humans.

"We can't let this island change," she said. "Ever. It's the only place left. The only place left." Then she gathered her clothes from the dock and sauntered back to her shack.

8

As I was wiping down the tables at the taverna in the early afternoon of the next day, Giannopoulos arrived together with Yannis the Red. They began playing backgammon, smacking the dice down on every roll as if the volume itself was critical. After only a few moves each, it became apparent that Yannis had a much stronger position. Of course, that meant nothing. Giannopoulos was probably letting him win.

As I made my way to their table with two glasses of ice and a bottle of ouzo, Giannopoulos said, "You're American." It was a statement. He lifted his eyes from the board for the first time and regarded me slowly. "You and your people have, for better and worse, changed the world," he continued, "turned it all into winners and losers, haves and have-nots. The winner takes all – the land or oil or fish, gets rich and calls it progress. That's exactly what Papakakis wants to do."

"Not all Americans think that way."

"Enough."

"I like the fishing life on this island."

"How long have you been here, again?" Giannopoulos smiled and leaned forward, elbows on knees.

"Long enough to know I want it to remain a marine reserve."

"My opponent, Papakakis, has money. He has connections. Those illegal nets he gives the fishermen, he doesn't buy them. They are given to him by people in Athens and other places, by people who have bought property here, who want the reserve status to be lifted and for development to start. It's a good strategy. They got in early, bought cheap, and know that when there are no fish left, no seals or dolphins or octopus left, then there will be nothing to preserve. Once we can no longer feed ourselves, the island will *have* to change, no matter what anyone thinks. Some people will make a lot of money."

Yannis glanced up and grunted his disapproval at this interruption in the game. Giannopoulos ignored him.

"Most of the fishermen are on Papakakis' side. It's not their fault. They have bought the big story, the one everyone tells – that restaurants, hotels, tourism is the way to a better life. They don't want to be left behind. The Reserve was already here, and it was working. There were enough fish, and people liked living here. The children stayed. The island was a success by any measure but financial. That was before Papakakis and his friends got their big ideas."

Giannopoulos took his turn but was already so far behind that it didn't matter. His pieces were piled on the middle of the board. He removed two with a hearty snap.

"My father was a fisherman who taught himself to read and write and became mayor," he said. "He saw what was happening all over the Aegean and he lobbied for a Marine Reserve here. It is his legacy. And he taught me to be proud to be a fisherman's son even as he sent me off to school in Oxford. When my British classmates were asserting royal heritage, I claimed my lineage as the son of a fisherman who was himself the son of fishermen. I trained to be an architect. I had big dreams, a folder of bold designs, and I even dated a

British girl, thin and pale as a codfish filet. She was almost see-through when the sun was behind her." He sighed.

"When my father died, I came back and realized how much I loved the island. How much I wanted it to stay the same. I did my best to preserve it while still in London, sent money back once in a while, but one day I began to understand how selfish that was. I wanted the island to stay the same for *me*, so that I could do grand things in London and have this place to come back to. I wasn't doing it for the right reasons. Who needs another pretty building? The Queen?"

He laughed dryly and picked up the dice. "If this place is worth preserving, if this life is worth preserving, then I had to be willing to live it. I had to prove it to *myself,* give up my life in London, break-up with my transparent Brit girlfriend, and come back here to live. Prove that it was worthwhile, and it is. It is! So that's why I am here, standing for a bloody election in which I have little or no chance. Now, I need to get back to this game, which I am also about to lose."

Kerryn was jumping off the dock when I broke through the tunnel of trees that night. Her body rose up and paused ever so slowly at the apex where, for a brief moonlit spell, she was a picture of freedom and release, before she fell headfirst into the water. She climbed the ladder and dove again before she noticed me. This time she put in a half twist. Moments after she surfaced, Yukon bounded from the water in a large orbit and likewise twisted half way around.

Kerryn waved for me to join them. I hesitated, but Yukon's appeal proved irresistible. I removed my clothes and stood at the edge of the dock, looking into the black sheet of water. I jumped in, then re-emerged at the surface. The next instant,

Yukon's long and sleek body swam a few feet in front of me. She slipped beneath the water, then circled back and passed me again, this time closer. She repeated the same pattern a third time, and I touched her with my fingers.

"Relax. She can sense what you're feeling," Kerryn said.

I tried to calm myself down, to tread the water smoothly while I waited for Yukon's next pass. She somehow sensed what I wanted. She came up between my legs and paused at my chest. I put my arms around her and, with a slight tinge of fear, locked my hands together on the other side, somewhere between her mouth and pectoral fins. My hands barely reached – Yukon was thicker than she looked at a distance – but I took a firm hold. Then there was a brief hesitation, a slight pull-back, just before she pulled forward.

"Hold on," Kerryn called.

We accelerated toward the edge of the cove, water pulling at my shoulders, wind whipping at my ears. Long ripples of muscles descended through Yukon's entire body as we gained speed, tearing through the sea. In a second, we were beyond the cove, looping up and down, bounding in and out of the water. In no time at all, I fell into rhythm, alternatively gasping for air as we leaped, then holding my breath as we dove, and this way we looped into the middle of the wide Aegean.

It was there, in the middle of the sea, that a wild utterance escaped my mouth, and as it did, something deep inside me was released. Whatever it was – pain, or guilt, or distress, I couldn't say – but it'd started as a sort of hot object in my chest and gut and grew until it expanded into my entire being, burning into my legs and head and hands. Then, almost instantly, like a dislocated bone snapping into place, the discomfort disappeared and was replaced by an almost sensual relief. We soared through the dark water, rapidly, deftly, chasing moonbeams. My arms clasped around Yukon, I closed my eyes and was grateful and blessed and holding on with all my might…

It all ended too soon. When I opened my eyes, I was looking at the approaching cove. Kerryn was beaming when we reached the dock, and Yukon rolled over and deposited me in the water.

"Wow," I said. "That was –"

But she didn't hear me. She was already off on Yukon, leaving nothing behind her but a rippled swirl near the dock. They emerged a hundred yards away, entwined, as if they composed a single gray and white body. They twirled, rolled and corkscrewed across the surface. Kerryn was pulling herself up and down on Yukon's body, falling back toward the fin on one rotation, pushing forward on the next. They circled the cove, and she started moving faster, up and down on Yukon like a bronco rider. As they closed in on the dock, Kerryn's grip tightened, and she opened her mouth as if to call out but swallowed a mouthful of water. Yukon stopped abruptly and Kerryn, flushed, was on top of her, laughing and coughing at the same time.

"Okay, that's enough," she said to Yukon. "I can't take it anymore."

With a chirp, Yukon's dorsal fin knifed its way out of the cove as Kerryn climbed the steps. She rubbed her head and eyes with the red towel then carelessly flung it over the rest of her body. She replaced the towel on the ladder and, still largely wet, took my hand as I grabbed my clothes. I remained exhilarated, my limbs tired, my heart pounding as we walked hand in hand back to her shack. Once inside, I put on my clothes and sat on the bed. Kerryn lit a tiny candle near the wooden desk, pulled on her white tee shirt and sat down next to me.

"I've never experienced anything like that," I said.

"Now you can understand why in Ancient Greece it was a capital offense to kill a dolphin. I told Papakakis that if this were a few thousand years ago, he'd be swallowing hemlock for what he's doing."

"When'd you tell him that?"

"Today. Those nets he has, dolphins can get caught in them."

In the spectral light of the candle, her features were softened and rounded. I put my hand on her knee as she started to cry. But the tears stopped almost as soon as they started. She held them back, steeled herself from emotion. I wiped a loose strand of hair away from her eye.

The candle was almost out by now, and the last of the flame spattered patterns of light on the far wall like a mercurial Rorschach test. She lay down on her side, propping her head up with one hand and crossing her ankles. I lay across the bed with her.

"Yukon and me, I thought we'd found the one place here, you know," she whispered. "It's supposed to be a Reserve, no large nets, no modern techniques, just the same fishing that's always been done. I don't know what to do anymore. I have to stop Papakakis, stop the nets, stop everything. But sometimes, I just get so tired. So very tired…"

A final tear leaked out as she closed her eyes. Not long after, her breathing grew shallow. Slowly, I pivoted her body so that she was lengthwise on the bed and lifted her head onto the pillow. She curled without waking and placed two praying hands beneath her lower cheek. I looked for a sheet to cover her, but she was lying on the only one. All I could find was an old beach towel under a pair of shorts on the floor.

For a few long, guilty moments I let my eyes linger on her body, tracking down the line of her neck to that tiny indented oasis, wet with sweat, where her collar bones almost met and over the small rounded breasts fallen sideways in her shirt. In time, my gaze came to rest on the long patch of stomach below her navel. I could feel my eyes narrow as I stared, feel a change start to take hold, an icy disengagement, and I didn't allow myself to look lower, tried to pull my thoughts away. I recalled my strange, thrilling ride on Yukon to rid myself of the growing want and accompanying detachment and indifference. No, I thought, this is not why I came to the island, and I glued my eyes right to the spot, no lower, staring at that golden hollow of skin, and daring, just once, a delicate finger over the bisect of fine, sun bleached hairs running down.

Eventually, I shook off the cold shiver that ran through my body and, by force of willpower alone, pulled the beach towel over her and let myself out the shack.

9

I lay awake for hours in my shack. Kerryn was a distraction and to let myself go any further was, I felt, a risk. She was enticing and alluring in the water and in her bed, but I was like an alcoholic staring down a drink: one taste of her golden, sea-logged skin could, I feared, trigger psychological and temperamental changes, perhaps beyond my ability to control. For the most part, I'd successfully held off the smirking man since I'd come to the island, and if I ever hoped to become again like the boy I'd been – wholesome, considerate, believing in God's infinite mercy – then I had to continue to resist his insidious inducements…

The alarm comes in just after 2:00 am, and we know it's a big one. We're sudden to awake and tense as we roll out of bed and dress. A brutal day in February – and perhaps it only feels this way in retrospect – but there had been something in the thinning air that whole white and ominous winter, the sense that all of New England was hunkering down for a reason.

We gather into the trucks, which rumble out of the station and into the night, our lights flashing like Christmas ornaments in the passing windows of the cityscape. Ahead, the Captain, who's been on the radio, looks back. He looks tired, as always, and his movements are slovenly and somber. He searches us with heavy-lidded eyes but says nothing. He doesn't have to. We know we're going in hot and high and deep. There's one every winter. It's the price we pay for sitting outside the station on all those summer days, working class hero-truants trading locker room jokes. It's the cost of all those women guided effortlessly into our beds.

For a night like this. A fire like this.

The first thing I notice is the height of the building. I'm afraid of heights, though this is something I've tried very hard to keep to myself. It's not an asset for a firefighter, of course. So I keep my white knuckles hidden whenever riding a Ferris wheel, or sky lift, or glancing over the far edge of a building. If anyone in the firehouse knew or suspected this fear, I'd be made to stand at attention from the station roof or eat lunch on the top of the engine's ladder.

I breathe a sigh of relief when I see the triple-decker. Though besot with risks, it's a building every Bostonian and fireman knows well: bay windows on the first and second floors, metal fire escape in rear (usually in some state of disrepair), firewall between every two buildings, a single staircase up one side of the interior. Forced heating, many of them, with heat pumps on the roof. This is how we choose to house ourselves, the cold, wooden architecture of northeastern lives.

The fire is well fed; some sort of propellant exists in the building, an unused oil burner, or wood or gas pipe. We see flames in several windows, but the building feels empty – another relief. This means we won't have to enter the building – not put our own lives at risk – as long we can keep the fire from spreading. And we can do that. We know we can do that.

The truck pulls up the street, siren down, the lights lighting up the windows of the buildings. A few faces, a few open windows, the usual crowd on the street in pajamas and overcoats.

We descend from the truck with studied, slow but exacting movements. I tighten my coat, pull my helmet tighter, wait for orders. Some men start moving the hoses toward the building to begin spraying into the windows. A ladder is raised to the roof as a precaution, though none of us think it'll be used. Steve, Ben Roper and I watch the Captain talk on the radio. We don't expect anything too much; the delivery of equipment somewhere, help with a hose. We expect to be back at the firehouse in two hours: Steve calling Francesca, Ben and I observing sleeplessly.

A moment on the phone, and the Captain looks at us flatly – the same look he'd given us in the truck. Twenty years on the force, and somehow he'd known about this one. I see him count with his eyes – one, two, three – something he could've done at a glance but he visibly counts us again – one, two, three – as if he needs to be sure. I can almost hear him thinking: three go in, three come out. He calls us over and tells us they suspect a homeless man on the third floor. Probably passed out, which could be a good thing if he's on the floor and not inhaling the smoke.

We pull on masks, helmets and oxygen and head into the building.

Fire is savage, spiteful, malevolent. A tiny, angry spark grows until it changes the weight and substance of surrounding objects. They lose mass – something our science teachers told us was not possible. And yet: wallpaper drips, plastic melts, walls become powder. A great reduction into indistinguishable goo and ash. But there is something comforting here, in the midst of the moaning, crackling and crumbling of the burning building. For here, in the great reduction, in this orange tinged darkness within the boiling onslaught and toxic odor, I'm endowed with a sense of peace. It may be the peace of hell, I'm aware, but often at these times, I'm compelled to stop and let contentment overtake me as an alter awareness manifests itself, one that goes to the heart of something I can't understand, when it is enough to wallow in this sanctity of destruction and enlightenment.

I don't want to make too much of this, for it may be no more than fear, the rush of meeting a power greater than myself, accept-

ing it, yielding to it. Yet, at times like these, I stand apart – above – beyond my fellow firefighters, my brothers, huffing and sweating and swearing next to me. The things I profess to these men – to enter and leave together, guard their lives above my own, never leave a man behind – are lies. In the heaven and hell of the heat and dark, in the midst of the melting, booming and crackling, I'm overcome with wonder and unearned superiority, as if I possess some special knowledge.

Steve goes in first, followed by Ben and myself. Steve bounds up the six concrete stairs to the front door like a kid to a roller coaster. The fact that he has the most to lose – neither Ben nor I have any responsibilities toward anyone but ourselves – is not considered. We've been trained, we've been paid, and we have a job to do. First among equals, Steve will do his. I follow him to the front hall which is an opaque grey cut only by the reflected flashing orange of an emergency light. The horn whales intermittently through my mask and helmet, partially muted. Within the bleating my heart thumps. Sweat bakes stiff on my body.

We round the steps to the first floor. The door to the unit is shut. I seek an excuse to return to the truck, to slip away and find something – mask, oxygen, axe – we may have left behind. But no; we're prepared. I pant, try to find a way to back out.

We go higher in the building, second floor, third floor. Darker. The heat is a furnace, knocking me back with a blow. Another emergency light on the third floor, misty orange through the smoke. We approach. A small landing and then a door. The alarm is persistent and loud. We gather on the landing.

Steve feels the door with his glove. He looks at me through his mask, and I know what this means: we're going in. There's no question in his eyes, and I know he hasn't considered the alternative of saying it's too hot, too dangerous and turning around. He could say he did it to save us; he couldn't risk our lives. But that's not who Steve is, not so much brave as dutiful, not so much principled as faithful servant. I'm his best friend and buddy, and I'm sure he's never entertained the thought that I wasn't exactly the same. It is, to him, the only way.

Opening a door is perilous. A suffocating fire is a desperate fire, gasping, inhaling, frantic as a drowning man. Steve begins to rock on his feet — one, two, three — and smashes the door. A boom. A leap of heat, light. Smoke and darkness and ashes, a flash of orange, a small beeping sound. The building has been baking; the supports will be weakened; this is a place to die.

A look back and Steve enters the room, one step, followed by Ben. I'm next. I don't move. Steve is lost ahead, Ben a fading silhouette. I wait on the landing, a torrent in my veins, watching my buddies disappear when it hits: peace in the chaos, wonder and awe. A cool, sublime feeling. Profound indifference. I feel safe somehow. Calm. I am fully the smirking man, once again, a hyper-consciousness. I will survive. Already I'm finding excuses, reasons my friends don't see me inside the room. Did I stumble? Take a wrong turn? Catch my mask on the frame? I consider lifting my mask and inhaling smoke to make it believable. Enough smoke and I pass out, risk death.

I'm not going in. My shadow consciousness, cold and removed, emerges, standing outside, above it all, not going in. I hear a crack from deep in the unit, a slight tremor beneath my feet. The stairs are reinforced. I'm determined to remain here, where there is support. I feel nothing but the need for my own survival, the famine victim hoarding bread from his family, watching them starve, letting them die.

I'm crude. Limbic. Rational.

I hear the telltale fracturing in the floor and know it may be the end of Steve and Ben. I can probably ride it out on the staircase. Steve and Ben will fall, break, burn. Despite my promises, I won't be with them. Though I could make a difference perhaps, a hand to hold, a carry out, I won't. In front of me, inside the door, the floor collapses. Breaking wood. Pealing plaster. Cracking cement. Dust and flashes. I hear a grunt, as if someone's been punched in the chest. The floor falls away like an elevator descending. I pray the staircase will hold.

Hail Mary, full of grace…

Smoke, dust and flames puff up from somewhere and surround me. I collapse as if cut at the knees.

Blessed art thou…

The heroes, Steve and Ben are gone and, on my knees, I am indeed apart – above – beyond. I crawl, my legs hurt, but appear to be intact. Have I been unconscious?

Holy Mary, Mother of God…

Footsteps somewhere distant, a voice calling. I feel relief, yes, but more than that, satisfaction, elation, a sense victory. As if I've won something. Two men down, and I alone alive, the smirking man who has endured, conquered, prevailed – all I know.

The cove is still as a graveyard in the deepening night when I – guilt-ridden, disillusioned, saddened, and grateful to be alive – finally withdraw into sleep.

A lynch mob was all I could think of when I saw the mass of fishermen gathered in front of Papakakis' taverna – a twisting, angry throng, fitful and fuming and hurling insults. Old women, furious and wild-eyed, lined the road behind the men, emitting series of long wails. In front of my own taverna was almost a mirror image of these groups, the men and wives, except they were calmer. Giannopoulos, Ari, Harry and the rest of them wandered about in a small area off to the side, hands in pockets, furtively glancing at their rivals. Their wives bustled in the rear.

It was a standoff, both groups waiting for something to happen, every fisherman and his wife alert for an inciting incident: a thrown rock, the wrong insult or gesture.

Then I saw it. In the harbor, five fishing boats sunk so low that only the pilot's houses – the small rectangular compartment that rose from the middle – remained above the water line. Large planks of curved blue wood floated listlessly, surrounded by buckets, cups, fishing gear and splinters. All the sunken boats were on the Papakakis side of the harbor.

Martin approached me. He had circles under his eyes and looked as if he had never seen this hour of the day before. He stared me down.

"Knew something like this would happen," Martin said. "Should've said something."

"I was with her last night."

Martin cast a skeptical eye in my direction. "A woman saw her on the boats in the early mornin', and Papakakis just went to talk to her. They'll find out soon enough. Feckin' stupid thing to do."

I stared at the flotsam in the harbor and knew in my marrow that neither Giannopoulos nor Harry, nor Ari, nor any of the other fishermen could have condoned an act like this, much less committed it. It had nothing to do with the election, nothing to do with any rivalry on the island. For no matter what tore these men apart, something stronger bonded them together; their fates were forever intertwined. I wheeled around and sprinted down the dusty road toward the cove.

When I broke through the tunnel of trees, Kerryn was sitting on the edge of the dock, as if she had been expecting me. She regarded me dispassionately as I approached. I was the first to arrive.

"Did you do it?" I asked. An obvious question to which I already knew the answer, but, for some reason, it seemed important to get her to confess it.

She didn't answer me.

"Did you do it?" I repeated.

She remained still, as if she hadn't heard me. There was resoluteness in her manner, a stiffness I'd never seen before. I squatted down to eye level.

"It's their island, not yours."

"Somebody has to stand up for the innocent."

"Who's innocent?"

"Yukon, the cove, all of this –" She extended one hand quickly to the sea.

"You can't just destroy their boats."

"I was saving the innocent. I was saving the island –"

"Damn it, Kerryn!"

We heard them at the same time, angry Greek voices carrying in from the dusty road, coming our way. I could sense the rumble of feet on the path. It wouldn't be long now.

"Get out of here," I said. "Hide. Take Yukon."

She looked at me, her deep set eyes hard against the sun, "There's nowhere to go," she said flatly.

A thin man with long sideburns had broken through the tunnel of trees, trailed by a mob of angry men. *"Nati!"* the side-burned man said, pointing at Kerryn

The men behind him quickened their pace and overtook him, hurrying onto the dock. It was like an invasion force, assaulting the tranquility of the cove. The combined weight of the men strained the supports of the dock; the planks creaked under their feet, the supporting pillars leaned to one side. I rose up, thinking the dock would collapse. Throughout all this, Kerryn didn't move, didn't even seem to notice.

A short muscular man in a sweat-stained shirt arrived first.
I stood in his way, but twenty men were behind him; they
passed me on both sides. A tallish fisherman grabbed Kerryn
under the arms and slung her up to her feet. Another one
held her hands back and tied them with a small rope. Kerryn
offered no resistance, simply let herself be lifted and bended
and tied. I tried to go to her and offer some sort of protection, but three other men, all from Papakakis' taverna, stood
in front of me. The side-burned man came forward and, with
a wave of his hand, motioned for the men to lead her out of
the cove. I remained alone on the dock as the grunts, shouts
and footfalls of the men faded away.

Abruptly, the cove was restored to what it always had been:
a glassy sheen of sea, serene breeze, green weeds, tress and dirt.
I could stay, I thought. I was safe here and had no obligation
to Kerryn or to anyone else. But as I felt the heat rise off the
planks of the dock, I was reminded of my cowardice on the
landing I'd never left in that triple-decker in Boston. In order
to banish the pain and guilt of that recurring memory – or
because I was growing more attached to Kerryn than I was
willing to admit – I headed to the village.

A crowd was waiting when I arrived. The women from
both tavernas lined the dusty road, leaving a thin path for the
circle of men with Kerryn to pass through. Across the way,
Giannopoulos and the other men squinted in the afternoon
sun. They hadn't bothered to come to the cove, had merely
waited for events to unfold. Now, Papakakis stepped into the
middle of the road and called out. He stood with his arms
folded, his feet planted firmly in the dirt. A gap opened up in
the circle of men holding Kerryn, and she was shoved forward.

Giannopoulos came over and stood next to me.

"Who's that man?" I asked, gesturing at the side-burned
man.

"Stephanos," he answered. "She sunk his boat and many others."

Kerryn stood in front of Papakakis, staring at him, challenging him. Papakakis hesitated for only a moment and then slapped her across the face with a broad swing of his hand. The smack rang out across the village and with that, the crowd found their collective purpose. Hurling insults, they surged in behind Kerryn. Papakakis stepped aside, and Kerryn was hustled down the road. She was jostled from behind; one fisherman tried to trip her; another spit on her; a woman reached out and ripped off the sleeve of her shirt. Kerryn kept her eyes down and, whenever she stumbled, jeers and laughter rang out from all sides.

Stephanos led her to an abandoned store on the far side of the soccer field. He untied her hands and then shoved her inside the little building. Papakakis quickly locked the door behind her, checked it twice, and then walked away.

I went to the front window of the store and peered inside. She was imprisoned in a one-room building that was empty, save for a single shelf against one wall, on which sat three soup cans and a box of laundry detergent. There was one other window that faced the soccer field on the opposite side of the room. Both windows were small with inch-wide metal slats running vertical to the ground.

"Anything you need?" I called to her. It occurred to me then that I might be her only friend in the world.

"Fine," is all she said and then, "maybe some water. I'm thirsty." Her eyes were moist as she looked up at mine, and she blinked slowly to hold back the tears. I don't know what she expected for her crime – I don't know what I expected – but it wasn't this. It wasn't to have her tied up and dragged to an abandoned store in the middle of the village. But the men of the island probably didn't have any idea what to do with her themselves, and this was the best they'd come up with.

I wasn't sure if she was really thirsty or was just looking for some sign that someone still cared, that someone was looking out for her. The reason was immaterial, of course, and I got a large bottle of water from the taverna. When I returned, she was rubbing her arm where the sleeve had been ripped off and seemed to have regained some of her composure, which I thought remarkable given the circumstances. I handed the water through the window.

"Maybe I shouldn't drink this. There's no bathroom in here."

"Wait," I said.

By this time, the men had started to disperse, and the women begun retreating into the inclined passageways that led to their homes. I went in search of Giannopoulos and found him standing on the side of the dusty road, engaged in a heated discussion with Papakakis. They stopped talking when they saw me.

"There's no bathroom," I said.

"She will be using the floor," Papakakis said.

"That's not right."

"Give her something," Giannopoulos said.

"Why? She will be ashamed? Is that it? She should be ashamed. I am finished with her. You tell the fish-woman, there is no bathroom…"

"She must have a bathroom," I said. "I'll report it."

Giannopoulos turned to me and raised his eyebrows.

"Report it?" Papakakis laughed. "To who? To me? Okay. I take care of it then." Papakakis thought for a moment, then smiled to himself. "You will wait here," he said and walked in the direction of his taverna. It was a small thing, the bathroom, but I felt I had to make a stand, thought it was important for Papakakis to know that someone, anyone was looking out for Kerryn.

"What will happen to her?" I asked as I stood alone with Giannopoulos.

"That is what we're talking about. Papakakis wants her to go to Athens. Pay a fine, go to jail and be exiled from the island and maybe Greece. She is the last person here from the group that came to help the animals. Papakakis wants to see her gone and is going to use this for every advantage to end the Reserve. He's already started. Did you see the scene in the village? That didn't have to happen. He wanted it to. He staged it. I have even less chances in the election now."

Papakakis returned holding a long thin bucket and handed it to me. The bucket was filthy and reeked of fish.

"Bathroom," was all he said.

I cleaned the bucket in the taverna before going to Kerryn's cell. The bucket was made of thin plastic and pliable enough to squeeze through the bars of the window.

"The comforts of home," she said.

I turned my back as she filled the bucket.

"Now what do I do with this?" she asked when I turned back. Her voice was calm, modulated, as if she greeted her new situation with complete indifference.

"Give it to me." I said.

Gingerly, I bent the bucket, now warm and yellow, back through the window, and took it across the dusty road toward the harbor. Kerryn's indifference, her demeanor, confounded me. She was so kind and easy going, so simple and gentle – except when it came to Yukon. The things she said about Yukon were easy to believe in the isolation and beauty of the cove, but in the heat and sweat of the village the perspective changed. Life was an elemental and uncomplicated struggle here; things were stark and simplistic, like the bucket of urine in my hand. I went to the far side of the harbor and emptied it.

"I've got to get to work," I said when I returned.

As the day went on, I checked on Kerryn whenever I could. For most of the day and into the night, she sat Indian style in the far corner of the room. A few times I looked in and, sitting silently, she never even knew I was there. Other times, I brought her water then some bread and then a green blanket and a pillow for her to sleep with.

"I'll stay here tonight if you want," I told her later, "I'll sleep in the taverna." She wouldn't hear of it; she insisted I go back to the cove to check on Yukon.

"There's a jar of dried fish in my room," she said. "Take it out to the dock and throw her some."

When I finally closed the taverna and went to check on her for the last time, she was already asleep. I decided not to wake her and simply left her there just as she was, alone and imprisoned.

I found the jar of fish in a cabinet in Kerryn's shack next to a bag of marshmallows and took it with me to the dock. It was a warm, star filled night with a dash of coolness when the wind picked up. I called Yukon's name, slapped my hand against the water and did my best to re-create Kerryn's shrill whistle, searching the outskirts of the cove for the dorsal fin cutting through the water. As if materializing out of my desire, Yukon was there, cutting towards me.

She arrived at the dock emitting a low hum. I think I understood what she was saying – she wanted Kerryn – but didn't know how to explain that she couldn't come. I sat on the dock and stared at her long sleek body. Kerryn had been our interpreter and, without her, we were strangers. We watched each other closely, searching for signals, differ-ent species with a common cause but no means of communication. I reached out tentatively and petted her. Yukon moaned again, and the permanent smile seemed to disappear from her face.

I removed a fish from the jar and held it in my hand. Yukon spotted it and dipped beneath the water. A few seconds later, she sprang up with a rusted soda can in her mouth. She flicked the can onto the dock and waited open-mouthed until I tossed her the fish. Next, she brought a small child's leather shoe up, and I rewarded her again. For some time after that, she swam slowly below me, circling solemnly and emitting a mournful low-pitched moan. Then she bobbed in the water, chirped once and took off.

Inside Kerryn's shack, I looked at her few remaining possessions: clothes and washing materials, cups and towels, paper and pens. Each of these everyday things, having been chosen so carefully, had become more precious. Despite the fact that her shack contained so few things – or maybe because of that – it contained a warm lived-in feel that my own lacked. And when the faintest familiar scents of her room, of wood and sand and sea, made themselves known, I lay on the floor and stared at the walls until, somehow and sometime later, I fell asleep.

I woke at the sun's first wink. Yukon was already in the cove when I went outside, exploring the area beneath the dock. She held a piece of old newspaper in her mouth by the time I reached the dock. I took it and threw her a fish from the jar I'd left there the night before. Seconds later, she dove down and brought up another piece of newspaper. I threw her another fish. We did this three more times. Then, as Yukon went to look for even more things, I jumped in the water again to see where she was finding all this trash in the otherwise pristine water. Under the dock, I spotted Yukon with a whole sheet of newspaper. Only she wasn't bringing the whole piece but tearing a little portion of it off each time. I took a breath, swam down and grabbed the entire sheet of paper. When I came back to the surface, she was long gone and presumably happy, having played me for a fool.

10

In the equatorial heat of midday, I arrived at Kerryn's cell. She rose stiffly from her cross-legged sitting position and came to the window. Her hair was oily and matted, her cheeks streaked with dried mud. A thin layer of dirty sweat covered her arms and legs, and her deep-set eyes appeared to have darkened and receded even further, giving her an owl-like appearance. Slow moving and dull-eyed, it was as if she'd morphed into the sad, sick, older sister of the woman I'd known in the cove.

With an unspoken apology, she handed me the bucket and looked away. Wordlessly I took it and, as I dumped the contents in the harbor, I recalled the Kerryn of the open cove: the single drop of water tickling down her back, her proud, almost defiant walk, her fearless, wild rides on Yukon – events that seemed so long ago. That in the course of one day I'd become the de facto protector and caretaker for Kerryn hadn't escaped my notice. I didn't want this position, but there was no possibility of abandoning her now. After our brief days and nights together at the cove, with and without Yukon, I wasn't sure if I could leave, even if I wanted to.

Back at the cell, Kerryn asked for a toothbrush, more water, candles and matches, a pen and paper, and some fruit.

"Necessities," she said, "nothing more. No more than ten items."

I gathered the items and, an hour or so later, found Papakakis, who reluctantly opened the front door, so I could pass through the requested items, as well as a chair I'd taken from the taverna.

Though it was mid-afternoon, I delayed opening the taverna. I was in no hurry to face the fishermen, whatever mood they might be in. Despite the heat, the kids' soccer game had started on the field. I bought one of those rotten cold coffees from the bemused girl at the grocery store and pulled a chair of my own below the window of Kerryn's cell. She seemed to have regained some of her former vigor in the meantime; the luster in her eyes appeared to have returned, if perhaps a little dimmer. As I sat on the chair, I told her how Yukon had tricked me into getting many fish with a single piece of paper.

"How many people could've thought of that?" she said, re-energized. "I've spent a lot of time with Yukon, and she's a whole lot more than smart. She *knows* she's alive, maybe not exactly in the way we do, but she's *conscious* of her existence in some way. That's why dolphins save people; that's why they get happy and depressed, why they play and are the artists of the sea. The joy of life. Yukon possesses a soul, as well. At least as I understand it. And it's these three things, intelligence, consciousness and a soul, that humans use to excuse their superiority over some animals. But dolphins aren't less than humans, just something other, more innocent and more enlightened. Somebody has to look out for them."

"Somebody... meaning you."

I turned around and rose to the window. She smiled and just then, behind her, under the green blanket I'd brought the day before, I saw something move.

"I think there's a rat under your blanket," I said.

She laughed, but didn't turn around.

"I'm not kidding," I said. "There's something under the blanket."

She went to the blanket and stood over it, her hand clasped on the corner.

"I wouldn't."

"You wouldn't, but I will," she said and, with a magician's flourish, whipped the blanket off the ground. And there, red-furred and fuzzy was Bobby, Martin's dog, his moist eyes staring at me as the blanket parachuted to the floor behind him. Bobby patiently waited for the blanket to settle to the floor and neatly burrowed beneath it once again.

"Keeps me warm at night," Kerryn said. "Martin lent him to me."

"I wouldn't have expected Martin to be so sensitive."

"He also gave me this," she held up a Bible. "He said it was the only book he could find in English."

"That's very nice of him."

"We go back, me and Martin."

Our eyes met, and I was flushed with the knowledge of something I didn't want to know. I suffered a gnawing sensation, a borrowing of dread in my gut. Could there have been something between them? I would've thought it impossible, but as I glanced at Kerryn, she nodded ever so slightly to confirm my suspicions. Martin? It was more than their ages that made it inconceivable. Martin was so wizened and fatigued, and she was so fervent and vigorous, that the two seemed not just incompatible, but impossible. But it was more than that. I'd assumed, if subconsciously, that Kerryn's only possible emotional involvement on the island had been Yukon, that there would've been no room for anyone else.

"You and Martin? How long did it last?"

"Not too long. I was, well, extremely lonely. I didn't know how to deal with that then. He's got that dark Irish charm, you know."

Maybe that was part of it; maybe I was threatened by Martin's charismatic world-weariness. More likely, it was that another man on the island had *possessed*, had *known* Kerryn. (It was precisely those pious, archaic terms that fixed in my mind.) I felt envious and angry, but also distant, one step removed, as if the emotions were happening to myself and someone else at the same time. I wondered if I had thought Kerryn unknowable, not possess-ible. Had I endowed her with a purity or sacredness and, by doing so, convinced myself that I might've finally arrived at my cloistered temple in the cove? Was that why I'd never tried anything physical with her? Or was it because some time ago I'd promised myself I'd stay away from intimacy as penance for the mentality I was now trying to rid myself of: ownership, possession, domination? The truth was that, like so very many things, I didn't know.

I avoided Kerryn's eyes. I felt as if some great possibility had been taken away, knowing full well that nothing had changed, and that I of all people deserved this. She wrinkled her brow. The sun gleamed in her dark eyes. "Martin was on the run, and I was too, in a way. We both spoke English…"

"I've an idea what Martin might've been running from," I said, "but not you." I struggled to catch her eye.

"Me? I wasn't running. Searching may be a better word, if it's not too pretentious. I was searching."

I adjusted my chair in the shrinking shadow of the cell wall. The strong smell of fish floated in a steamy breeze.

She went on. "I was searching for… somewhere. I don't really know. When I was a kid, a teenager, there was this animal shelter that opened next to the home where I lived. There were some people there, kind people, trying desperately to find places for animals so they didn't have to be euthanized. I started spending more and more of my free time there, helping them out, walking the animals or cleaning the cages. I fell in love with the animals, all of them, the sloppy dogs and independent cats, the skittish guinea pigs and hoppy little rabbits. We couldn't save them all, but we tried. We really tried. And in time, I began spending *all* of my time there, sleeping there every night, curled up next to the cages."

"What about your parents, didn't they care?"

"No, no, nobody cared. It was all right. It was good. I did go back to the house to clean up once in a while, but that was it."

On the field, some kid had scored a controversial goal, and there was a burst of cheers over the objections. Cold sweat ran down my arms as I finished the last of my coffee.

"But then the animal shelter ran out of money. We'd been surviving on donations, and they slowed down, and one day we just couldn't pay the rent. We closed up shop, and I was left with nothing to do and nowhere to go, so I joined the first animal rights group I could find. They were passionate and determined. I liked their spirit. After a few months saving turtles and the odd dog and cat, I heard some of them were organizing a trip to Greece to save monk seals and dolphins. I begged until they agreed to take me with them. We did some good work, saved a few seals and a few dolphins, but suddenly we were *invited* to leave, our welcome was revoked. I believe Papakakis had something to do with that. But by this time I'd struck up a special friendship with Yukon, and I wasn't going anywhere. So I stayed."

"With nothing."

"Almost nothing. I had Yukon and was, well, peaceful and content for the first time since I could remember. I felt like I was onto something here."

"Do you still feel that way? Is staying here and reducing your possessions doing what you thought it would do?"

She crinkled her nose as she thought about it. "I don't know yet. I think so, yes. But sometimes late at night, in the cove with Yukon, I feel like we're being preyed upon by an unknown and massive force. That it's all around us, wanting us, wanting what we have, wanting the cove, just ... wanting. I often wonder: can I live alone in a reserve, away from everyone, without being harmed and without doing any harm? Can anyone?"

It was reminiscent of my first few days, the way the fishermen treated me at the taverna. They gruffly ordered drinks and otherwise acted as if I didn't exist. I'm sure they assumed that if my girlfriend – and they most certainly assumed Kerryn was my girlfriend – could sink Papakakis' boats, she could sink theirs as well. I realized how little I'd done to integrate myself with the fishermen, what little I'd learned of this Greek island culture. I'd devoted my time and thoughts to the English speaking people on the island – Kerryn, Martin, Giannopoulos. This was a mistake, of course. If I'd come to get away from myself, one way to do it was to immerse myself in another language and way of life, but I'd not done that. And didn't see how I could fix it now, even if I tried. It was, simply, another failure.

On this specific day, the fishermen were busy with other things. One fisherman had managed to get a few unauthorized pictures of Papakakis and his wife, and Harry had come up with a plan. He left with the pictures and, in the time it took Martin to drink three beers, returned with tiny copies of the pictures and a couple of sticks of glue. He started in on Papakakis, blaming him once again for the lack of fish, then for the rough seas, the increased price of fuel, and the poor quality of this year's feta.

As the fishermen muttered in agreement – none of them had thought about the feta before – Harry removed a one hundred drachma note from his pocket. It had a picture of Giannopoulos' head above what looked like the body of a featherless chicken. Harry slapped this bill on the table and began outlining Giannopoulos' face with glue. Then, almost giddy, he took the tiny picture of Papakakis and stuck it on top.

In short order, the fishermen took out their own currency and began to glue Papakakis' face upside down and sideways, with mustaches and beards and other much less decent things. Then they pasted Papakakis' wife's face on top of a bottle of ouzo. They poked a hole in her mouth and started to pour through it, making vomiting noises. They were in no rush, the fishermen, and it was turning into a long night. I didn't care. I drank ouzo as I watched them, sipping the anise-flavored fog, first over ice and then straight. It went down smooth and easy, too easy.

Martin sat off to one side. I watched him for some time before I got up to bring him another beer. I was uneasy on my feet and did my best to walk a straight line to his table. When I pulled out a chair, it fell. I picked it up and sat down.

"You and Kerryn…"

"You and a lot of ouzo…"

"Didn't tell me," I said.

"Didn't ask."

"Never entered my mind."

"Nor mine."

"Are we going to move into complete sentences anytime soon?"

"Can you still speak one?"

"Yes."

"I know what you're after." He stared out the door, sipped his beer. "We've both changed a lot, sure. I've grown older. She may have gotten younger and, with that stunt, dumber." He lifted his hat, looked out the side of the wide brim – "Things could be worse, my friend" – then let it fall back. "It's not right what she's doing. An island is an island for a reason, and outsiders shouldn't be gettin' involved. Her heart's in the right place but so what? Guess I saw it comin', when she first got here, writin' all those letters about the nets, and standin' on the docks, talkin' to the fishermen, as if any of that could change their minds. She has somethin' burnin' inside her. Not quite anger, maybe, but somethin' like it. She tries to keep it hidden, to keep it buried deep down but, you know, somethin' happened to her in that home."

"What home? The home for animals? The animal shelter?" I felt foolish, even as the words left my mouth. If I'd only taken a moment to think about it, I'd've figured it out.

"She didn't tell?" Martin smiled. "Ah, but she wouldn't, would she? Didn't tell me either until I pried it out of her piece by piece. She was raised in foster homes. Never knew her parents but suspects they abandoned her. And the last foster home she lived in as she was gettin' older, well, somethin' happened to her there. Not sure exactly what, but it isn't so hard to guess, is it? Pretty girl like that."

A small tremor went through me. I glanced out the door so Martin couldn't see the shock in my eyes.

"That's why she spent so much time in that animal shelter," he went on. "That's what started her in with the animals. She doesn't like to be around people very much, and can't say

I blame her. She only let me in, and now maybe you, because, if you don't mind me sayin', we've both got somethin' of the wounded dog about us, don't we?"

"*Allo ouzo,*" I heard sharply behind me. I delivered it to the fisherman, who took it from me without a glance or word of thanks, and staggered back to Martin. This time I had my own bottle of ouzo in which there was less than a quarter left.

"Stuff'll sneak up on you." Martin said, pointing his chin at the bottle then asked, "eat anythin'?"

"Nope."

"Hope you make it to closin'." Martin thought for a long moment. He knew why I was drinking, must've sensed I needed a release and kindly tried to help. "Ever hear of The Maze? Long Kesh Prison? Useless as I seem, I do know a somethin' or two 'bout prisons – how to get in, which is easy, and how to get out, which is not. If you want, we could bust Kerryn out of that cell, squirrel her away in a lorry on some ferry, then hide her 'neath the floorboards in the houses of sympathetic animal lovers across the Mediterranean." He drank the rest of his beer down in one gulp.

"I'm serious."

"So was I, at one time. The reason I'm here."

I looked at him. He squinted and looked out the taverna door. "Well, you don't want her to be leavin' the island," he said, changing the subject. "When someone here is arrested, they send the paperwork to Athens to be processed. You need to stop that. If things go to Athens, forget it. Papakakis has connections there. Try to keep things local."

"How can I do that?"

"Talk to your man, Giannopoulos. Don't know what he can do unless he gets elected. But if he's elected, then he can do whatever the hell he wants."

"So I need to get him elected."

"You'd really need to join the CIA to be doin' that. Everybody here knows who they're votin' for, knew that decades ago."

"What can I do?"

"The only way to turn this thing is to get as many Giannopoulos voters onto the island as possible and keep most of Papakakis' lot away."

"People can return and vote?"

"In Greece, you vote where you were born. So that can help, but even that won't change the outcome."

"You're saying it's hopeless?"

"'Course it's hopeless. Everything's feckin' hopeless. Then again, Bobby lives, and who'd've bet a hangnail on him?"

I did make it to closing, barely, an oppressive headache already setting in before the last fisherman left. When he finally did, I closed the door behind him, lie on the floor and watched the ceiling spin until I passed out.

11

I awoke with a shiver on the cool taverna floor, my mouth parched and thick with the sickly aftertaste of soured ouzo. For a stretch of time I didn't move, staring with dry eyes at the ceiling, and sensing the floor move in a sickening, offbeat rhythm that jaggedly countered the throbbing in my head. Eventually, I rose from the ground and lost my balance, staggering into a table that scraped across the floor. I knew there was aspirin behind the bar and managed to choke one down with half a glass of water. I waited to see if I'd vomit it up, then headed out into the violently bright morning sun and made my way across the dusty field to Kerryn's cell.

She was in a deep sleep, curled around Bobby in such a way that the small green blanket covered both their bodies. It was already warm at that hour, and there was a glaze of perspiration on her neck and forehead. The skin of her left cheek touched the dirty floor and struck me as too smooth, too vulnerable to remain there. I regarded Kerryn in an entirely different light now, after the revelations of the night before. On the surface, it seemed to explain many things – the devotion to Yukon, the hermit-like existence in a foreign land, her seemingly sexless sensuality. Then again, what did I know about it? I was entirely out of my depth and abruptly realized how self-absorbed, and perhaps deluded, I'd been in my thoughts and dealings with her.

Inside the cell, Bobby twitched his nose and lifted his head. He lazily turned to me, licked his lips, then snuggled back against Kerryn and went to sleep. I got the impression he'd be happy to stay that way forever and wondered if, in her slumber, Kerryn was being carried back to the animal shelter of her youth, and if, like then, the warmth of a sleeping animal by her side offered a degree of kinship and protection she'd never found in the greater world.

I decided to let them both sleep and sat on the chair beneath the window to ride out my hangover. In time, the local kids gathered and started a soccer game on the field. Since I'd started watching these games, it had amused me that all the arguments broke out between players on the same team, over a missed pass or lazy defense, and rarely, if ever, between the players on opposite teams. It brought to mind Greek myths and theater and history, all the treachery involved, the endless betrayals and re-betrayals of the gods and leaders and warriors, smirking men all of them.

The boys' soccer teams were usually divided fairly and not in accordance with the political loyalties of their fathers. But I noticed there was always a small, desperate-looking boy that stood alone. Despite that, he seemed to live for the matches. Whenever anyone scored, from either team, he stomped his feet and raised his hands; when someone got hurt, he grimaced and held the wounded area on his own body. He never once played, though I couldn't detect any obvious physical restrictions, and none of the other kids ever talked to him. On this island he was effectively cornered. The choices were probably watch the game alone or stay at home bored.

The game that day was close – *thee-oh, thee-oh* for most of the time – and provided a needed distraction. There were entire stretches of time when I forgot about my hangover. Towards the end of the game, one of the better, older players named Vassilis received a pass on the right side of the goal. The goalie was out of position. With an explosion of dust and grunts, he let loose with a ferocious kick, then slipped and fell on his back as the ball flew five yards wide of the net. The goalie reached out a hand to help Vassilis up but pulled it away when Vassilis grabbed for it. Vassilis spat and swore as he rose to his feet. The boys on both teams were laughing.

By this time, the boy who stood all alone had retrieved the ball and was on his way back. Vassilis, humiliated, called to him: "*trexe, Pavlos, trexe!*" The others soon took up the chant, adding obscenities as this boy dribbled the ball back with his feet. He lacked some coordination and seemed barely able to keep the ball in front of him. I now knew why the boy didn't play, but he did serve his purpose. When he reached the field, Vassilis kicked the ball away from him and pushed him to the ground.

"*Fiye, ilithie, fiye apo tho!*" Vassilis screamed. The words were loud and cruel, and I had no trouble understanding them: "Leave, you idiot, leave from here!"

The boy, Pavlos, started trembling and looked at the rest of the players with pleading, watery eyes, hoping he wouldn't have to leave. Another player came between Vassilis and Pavlos, a younger player, no more than eleven years old. They called him Pete. He was a skinny kid but fast, and, as I'd seen, knew how to use his speed to great advantage.

"Leave him alone." Pete said.

"Why?" Vassilis yelled. "Why? He comes here every day. For what? He doesn't play. He's stupid." Vassilis pushed Pavlos again, this time with one hand. Pavlos, on the ground, started to cry.

"He gets the ball for us," Pete said,

Vassilis walked around Pete to Pavlos. I noticed he didn't touch Pete. Pavlos backpedaled like a crab, his thick arms and legs working furiously to carry him away from Vassilis. But Pavlos was not fast enough, and Vassilis grabbed him beneath his armpits, lifted him a foot in the air, spun him, and dropped him back down.

"Leave," Vassilis said, threatening Pavlos with a kick. "Draw your stupid pictures. Don't come back. Ever!"

Pavlos stumbled off with his head down, looking back with every step and, as he shambled away, I couldn't help feeling sorry for him, knowing he was trapped on this island, knowing he'd likely never get away.

By this time, the boats had begun filling the harbor. Kerryn was still sleeping, and I left the chair by her cell to open the taverna. My headache had subsided to some degree – whether that was the time passed, or the game, or the aspirin, I didn't know and didn't care. I was forcing myself to drink a glass of water when Pavlos arrived at the door. Wearing ripped knee length black shorts, a dirty white under shirt and old leather shoes without laces, he reminded me of a homeless man. His head was bowed, and there were tears in his sad eyes. He'd never been to the taverna before.

"Your name's Pavlos," I said. He seemed to be waiting for me to speak.

"Yes," he replied in English, staring blankly. He didn't move.

"Want something?"

He took a moment to think about this. "Yes. Alcohol," he responded, again in English. "This, I want. This, I need."

His English surprised me. The accent was heavy, as expected, but he seemed sure of his words. I commented on this.

"Yes, Americky television, I am watching, and in school, I am learning. I am not so good at sports. I speak English better.

You give me alcohol like British Special Agent 007, James Bond? Vodka martini, shaken not poured."

"Stirred."

"What?"

"I think you watch too many movies."

I poured him a mixture of Seven-Up and orange juice, widely known as a screw-up. Pavlos rested his chin on the edge of the bar between sips. As I swept the floor, he grabbed a napkin and started sketching with a thick pencil he had in his pocket. He drew in rapid and seemingly careless strokes, barely lifting his head from the bar, and was done not long after he started.

When I finished sweeping he asked, "May I tell you something?" Then he said in a matter of fact tone, "I do not know why everyone is so mean to me. This I do not know." With that said, he slinked out the door before the fishermen started to arrive.

He left the napkin for me to see. It was the sketch of a thin, solitary man – me – sweeping a cavernous taverna. Outside the door of the taverna, the sea rose ominously, as if a tidal wave was about to wash away the taverna and with it the whole island. Even though it was casually drawn, it revealed a keen eye and a skilled hand. Pavlos had played with the proportions so that the taverna looked much larger than it was, and I in turn seemed smaller, almost inconsequential. The more I looked at it, the more I thought that he had gotten it exactly right.

More than a few times that day, I studied the napkin, flattening it out on the bar or holding it up to the light. The drawing seemed to possess not just a unique perspective, but some sort of insight into the trifling, impermanent world of the island.

Later, when I was closing up the taverna, I threw it out. It didn't seem like much, something dashed off by a bored, if talented, island boy. It wasn't long until I'd realize the mistake I'd made in discarding that thin square of paper.

After Pavlos left, I bunkered down at the taverna with aspirin and liquids. The bright sun was searing and abrasive, and I didn't venture to Kerryn's cell until near dinnertime, when the taverna had emptied out. I promptly told her that, in the interest of full disclosure, Martin had offered to bust her out of the cell and sneak her away across the Mediterranean in trucks and boats. I added that if anyone could do it, he could, as he appeared to have some experience in the matter. Kerryn shook her head the whole time I was talking.

"Tell Martin, thanks, but I don't want to escape," she said. "I want to stay here and fight. I've already decided on my defense for the trial." She stroked Bobby's head on her lap.

"There's no defense," I said. "A lady said she saw you do it, and every man on both sides of the island will testify against you."

"The defense isn't why I'm innocent. It's why I'm *guilty*."

"I was afraid of something like that."

"I call it the garden defense." She smiled at the words.

I sighed. "I don't like it already."

"I've been reading this." She pointed at the Bible. "The Greeks are a religious people, Orthodox Christians, so I'm going to read from their own story. I started reading it myself, from the beginning, all about Genesis, Adam and Eve, Cain and Abel, the fall from grace. All of that good stuff."

"How's that going to help you?"

"It just jumped out at me, what it's about," she continued. "*Why* Adam and Eve fell and were cursed, *why* we fell from the garden, *why* Cain killed Abel, and *why* countries are divided, and *why* people are divided, and *why* this island is divided, and *why* and *why* and *why,* until finally *why* I sank the boats. It's a chain reaction."

I leaned my chair on an angle against the wall and sipped a glass of water. I knew all about being cursed, of course, having been thoroughly lectured on original sin. I didn't see how that could help her, but had to admit I was curious. "From Adam and Eve to you. Please tell me."

"The early stories, the first stories of the Bible, are stories of the transformation of society from a hunter-gatherer 'do-no-harm, take-what-is-freely-given' way of life to an agricultural 'work-the soil, accumulate-land-and goods' way of life. Adam and Eve had everything they needed, but they wanted more. They messed up, and their descendants – that's us, you, me, the fisherman, almost everyone – were *cursed* by God to scrape and dig and struggle to survive."

Her voice cracked and, keyed in by Martin, I sensed, for the first time, the suppressed emotion which weighted her words. I supposed this was what he'd alluded to when he said there was something burning inside her, a swell of feeling that she was afraid of or had learned, long ago, to suppress.

"What you say may be true, Kerryn," I said, "but I don't see how it's going to help you."

"Listen to what it says-" she picked up the Bible and flipped through the first few pages. '*The Lord God sent him forth from the garden of Eden, to till the ground from whence he was taken.*' This is it, right, so, Adam and Eve are banished from the Garden, where they had everything, and are forced to till the ground, to farm. Then later Cain, a tiller of the ground, kills his brother Abel, a shepherd, a hunter-gatherer, because God is not pleased with Cain's offering. God knows that the farmers will become too many. He knows the farmers will overwhelm the hunter-gatherers, killing them if they have to, until there is no place left for them. The Bible actually lists them, who begat who. It wants us to know. It goes on and on, for pages and pages. The beginning of the Bible is about agriculture and population growth as *destiny*, leading to inevitable territorial wars, as the need for fresh land overwhelms everyone and everything, until there is no place left to live simply and freely and without harm."

"Like in a reserve?"

"Like dolphins do. It's all right here in the Bible. The price we pay for Adam and Eve's desire, mankind's *desire*, the colossal expansionary threat that we've all lived under since Cain. Don't you see? I had to strike back, had to do something. So maybe, maybe, we could start again. We could make our way back."

She stopped abruptly as her voice cracked again, as if she was holding back that great swell of feeling. And I thought I began to understand why. In the beginning chapters of Bible, Kerryn had found an explanation for what had happened, not only to her, but to all of us – what had caused the sorry state of affairs among men. In those ancient words, in some way, she'd found the answer she'd been looking for since she was an orphaned and abused child.

"You mean, go back to the Garden of Eden?" I asked. "Is that what you're saying?"

"Not... exactly. Maybe, just, to the springtime in the garden of a few souls?" She smiled, then laughed at herself. "Who knows? Jesus never had anything; Buddha and Mohammed left all they had. They just did what they did, simply, with nothing, and eventually others heard and followed. Isn't that their example? Isn't that every true religious leader's example? So what I'm going to do is read these pages. Maybe a trial will be a blessing."

"First, I don't think they'll let you read the Bible at a trial and second, I don't think anyone, anywhere much cares what happens here."

"But if the trial is unusual in some way, it might lead to some publicity. Maybe others around the world will hear, maybe others are already doing it, finding a new way to live, and we don't know. Maybe you or Martin could write to a few papers or something and tell the story of the Reserve, the Bible, why the boats had to be destroyed."

"All they'll ever hear is the story of a crazy woman who sunk a few fishing boats on a Greek Island. You'll be labeled a lunatic. Another animal rights extremist."

"Someone, somewhere might listen to my defense."

"We're five thousand years into agriculture, into property and ownership and expansion and all that stuff, and you're going to argue for a return to some lost romantic ideal of hunting and gathering? I think you need a real defense."

"Is it idealistic and romantic or just a different way of thinking about a sustainable way of living? It's what the Bible is trying to tell us about where we all went *wrong*."

I felt compelled to deflate her expectations somewhat, if only so she wouldn't be too disappointed.

"We've gone too far in the other direction."

"That's why the time is right," she laughed again. "I know you think it's delusional, but there's nothing but interpretation, is there? That's all there is. About sustainable living, what should and shouldn't be preserved or owned, about God, and dolphins, and you, and me… it's all just interpretation. The way we see it." She smiled. "Change interpretation and you change the world. I intend to give my interpretation, that's all. See if it takes hold somewhere, somehow, with some person. That's all any of us can do."

A shooting star zipped across the sky. I watched it streak behind the mountain on the other side of the island as I thought about the woman against the opposite side of the concrete wall, so very different from me – or anyone. She was a genuine being, pure in spirit and without pretense, willfully removed from possessions, greed, artificiality, and guided, not by tradition like the fishermen, nor by desire or competitiveness as I'd been, but by her imaginings and passions and, to use her word, interpretations. Either because of or in spite of her past, she'd become a culture unto herself, far removed from anyone or anything I'd ever known and, for that, there was something uncorrupted and beautiful within her – unlike myself, the waste of a man beside her, who'd been given much and only wanted more, and who'd traded love and purpose for the grotesque satisfactions of a smirking man.

I turned around, reached for her dirty hand through the bars, and kissed it; and nothing in mind and memory seemed more honest, more true than this single kiss.

12

The next day at the taverna, the fishermen were a mixture of moods, none of them good. It'd been a poor day of fishing, all around, worse than usual. Most of the men claimed to have caught nothing, and those that had dismissed it as cat food. Yannis the Red had taken a table in the middle of the taverna and was drinking ouzo and seething. At one point, he abruptly stood up, kicking his chair to the ground behind him. He said he didn't know about anybody else, but he couldn't go on any longer. He couldn't catch enough fish to feed Liza, he said, and couldn't imagine what the men were doing for their wives and children. He spit on the ground.

Giannopoulos walked in when he was speaking and quietly took a seat near the door, but Yannis noticed him. "Let me tell you something, Kostas. I do not understand what we are doing here. I am hungry and I am tired. The others, over there, Papakakis' men, they are not hungry. They can eat and that makes them right."

Giannopoulos went to the center of the taverna and stood next to Yannis. He put his arm on Yannis' shoulder as he began to speak. "Many years ago, when I was a little boy, and everyone in this taverna was a young man, my father came up with the idea for a fund. Everyone contributed. Where would we be now without that fund?"

"The same place we are now." Yannis said, laughing ironically. "Poor and hungry." Some other men laughed as well.

Giannopoulos waited for the laughter to subside. Then he looked around the room, questioning every man with his eyes. They finally came to rest on Yannis the Red, standing just inches away.

"We are old, Kostas," Yannis said, almost as a whisper. "Too old to fight a losing battle."

"If we let things change, we will destroy ourselves. We will all be working in a hotel or restaurant, which is slavery for an old man who has been on the sea. Have you seen a fisherman who doesn't fish? The spirit of the man is broken."

"What spirit?" Yannis said. "We have no fish. They are sweeping them all away in their nets."

Giannopoulos nodded sadly. "But it's about more than us. We need to hold out, to prove to the world –"

"I don't give a shit about the world when I am hungry," Yannis said. The other fishermen men grunted in agreement.

"Look, this is *our* Reserve," Giannopoulos said. "It's not to save the few fish left, it's to save us. We are the last of our kind, simple fishermen, descended from the ancients, the sons of apostles of Jesus. And this place –" He stopped to catch his breath. "If we don't hold out, you know what comes next? Fishing trawlers and buildings everywhere and crowds and restaurants and pollution, and we will all disappear. Everything we know and love will disappear, without anyone knowing or caring that it was ever here. We'll be just another destination for the cruise ships. No different than any other island, anywhere. My great friends, we *have* to hold out." He spoke the last words quietly, almost hopelessly.

"For how long?" Yannis asked.

"Forever, I think, or until we die. This is our Thermopylae." Giannopoulos smiled to himself, as if acknowledging the immensity of what he was asking. "Here's what I'll do. If every man will tell me what he needs to make it, I will pay him that amount from the fund. No questions."

He glanced around the room, and one by one all the men nodded in agreement. Yannis the Red was the last person he looked at, and the large man shrugged helplessly, reluctantly.

"Okay, Kostas," he said. "I will give you until the election to see if you can win because you are a good man. But that is all I can give. No more. Not forever, because I will be dead before then."

Within thirty minutes each man had made his way over to Giannopoulos with the amount he needed to survive the next few weeks. Giannopoulos marked each amount on a piece of paper. When the men were done, I too strode over to him. He watched me approach with a look of dismay on his face, as if I were the last person he wanted to see – which I probably was.

"You want our money too?"

"Something else."

"Retsina first."

When I returned with the metal pitcher and a glass, he grabbed it and started talking before I could speak. "I have an idea what you want, CIA, and I would like to help you. I would. But there is nothing I can do."

"Talk to Papakakis."

"It wouldn't do any good. Your girlfriend said a lot of things and wrote some letters and tried to make life difficult for Papakakis in the last couple of years. He sees this as revenge."

"I want to stop the paperwork from going to Athens. Do you think he sent it?"

"My instinct tells me no. He's lazy but gets around to everything sooner or later. He's already started rumors that I made it happen. He's telling people that I planned to destroy the boats with the CIA, you and your girlfriend. So right now, I just have to step back and let things be."

"If you were elected, could you help?"

"I could try. I believe that woman means no harm to the island. But she'd have to pay for the damage to the boats. She has put us all in an awkward position. In fact, it is best if I am not seen talking to you for any length of time. So…"

My options were limited, and as the day went on, I debated the prospect of breaking Kerryn out of jail, pulling out a few of those loose bars on her window and fleeing. I doubted anyone would chase us. Only Papakakis would care, and he would be happy to get rid of us.

During these ruminations, it wasn't lost on me that, despite my best intentions, I found myself caught up in a number of personal and political entanglements. And that there was nothing I could do about it. I wanted Kerryn free, I wanted Yukon safe, and I wanted Giannopoulos elected. It felt like I'd arrived only a minute ago on the island, the stalwart pilgrim knowing nothing and no one. And now…

Then it occurred to me that, however unlikely, I still had one option left to help Kerryn – Papakakis himself.

Most of that afternoon, I stood in the doorway of the taverna keeping one eye on the men inside and another looking for Papakakis on the dusty road. I served the drinks quickly and returned to my spot at the door. It gave me time to think, and as I mulled over the sacrifice Giannopoulos was asking

the men to make, I returned to an exhibit of the firefighter I'd
been, smirking man and false hero…

*"You didn't go in?" Francesca's eyes are bloodshot. Her left fist
is clenched, fingernails digging into her palm. She hasn't let me
in the door. "How come you didn't go in?" She is screaming. I'm
standing outside the door of her third floor walk-up, where she
and Steve used to live.*

"Let me in."

*"I asked a question!" Still screaming, her face a stone, the
second generation Italian accent coming through.*

"The neighbors can hear —"

*"Fuck you, the neighbors. You didn't go in! I want to know
how come my husband died in that fire and you didn't. You think
I don't know?"*

*I push my way past her and into the room. I am too eager to
get through the door. My shoulder hits hers, knocks her back. She
stumbles back, almost falls, and I wonder if she's been drinking.
She spits at me. It lands on the leg of my jeans with a* thwat. *I
slam the door shut behind me.*

"Wait."

*"Fuck, wait." Her accent grows heavy and unattractive. "I
read the report and you come here." She wheels on me, raises a
hand to hit me, lets it fall.*

*"Did you plan it? Tell me, did you plan it? Get Steve out of
the way and take me like a whore. Let him die to get me." Her
face is suddenly old, her smooth dark features becoming sharper
and unappealing. She wants to hit me, raises her hand again, then
stops. The hate turns into something hard and small, like resolu-
tion. She's tough and has been through too much. She can't take
it anymore and withdraws into herself. As if she can't believe all
these things have happened, and the men she had known were men
like me. Cowardly, cruel, scheming men, taking what they can…*

Less than a week ago, I'd called to come over, asking her if she needed anything. We'd been getting closer in a series of phone calls and weekly comfort sessions. I'd come over to talk about Steve, to hold her hand, share a glass of wine, hug her. Things were more physical between us, more platonically intimate. I'd begun to tuck her into bed after long talks on the couch.

Steve was three months in the ground at this point, and I'd become a true working class hero, the sole beneficiary of all the grief and gratitude the city could offer to the men who'd given their lives.

The City of Boston was shut down from a numbing Nor'easter, which had blown through that day and dumped 18 inches of snow on the ground. I'd pulled a double shift at the firehouse when some of the guys couldn't make it in. I was pleasantly exhausted and looking forward to a few days off when I called Francesca. Something told me this was the moment – that the cold and snow set loose things that weren't otherwise loose. I knew it the second I opened the door.

"In the bath," she called.

The door wasn't locked. I walked into the apartment, placed a bottle of Chianti on the kitchen table and headed for the bathroom. I'd been thinking of her almost nonstop in the weeks prior, the smirking man scheming how to get into her black jeans. Francesca sat in the bath, telling me she'd been there for an hour... or two... she didn't know. She didn't have the strength to get out of the bath and had kept turning the hot water on so she wouldn't freeze.

"I don't think I'll ever get out," she said. The curtain was pulled halfway across the tub, covering her legs. There was a pack of cigarettes on the ledge of the tub, which surprised me. I didn't know she smoked. Something classical and melancholy was playing distantly in another room. I stood looking at her in the tub. She was leaning back, head against the edge with her knees to one *side and her breasts floating toward the surface. I kept my eyes on hers. She blinked slowly, pleadingly.*

"We'll get you out," I said.

"Is it still snowing?"

"Stopped a while ago."

"Can you help me get out? I'm afraid."

"Take your time. No hurry."

"There's a towel over there," She pointed across the room.

I grabbed a large bath towel and made my way back to her. She'd been drinking. I saw a tumbler with ice on the lid of the toilet. She was half drunk and fully lost, looking for a way out of the place she'd been since Steve died in the building I'd walked out of.

I lifted the towel from the corners with my arms out wide, ready to wrap Francesca up as I'd seen in a hundred movies. She rose from the tub blocked by the towel and came toward me. I dropped the towel and wrapped her in my arms. She was wet and smelling of some soft soap. Her skin was warm, and she lifted her face to mine. And I knew that I'd succeeded then, that one way or another I'd won. I was alive and taking full advantage of that. There was no remorse, no consideration for her vulnerability or what she might be experiencing. She was another naked woman in my arms – a woman I'd wanted for a long time, true, but just another woman to be known and possessed.

That was before Francesca read the report. Now she's discovered that I'd never entered that condo, that I'd waited outside while the others burned. (A close reading of the internal report reveals this, though I'm confident this specific information will never go public. I will remain the hero.) Francesca knows that I'd been standing on the landing before, during and after the collapse. That I'd slept with the wife of the man that I'd let die alone there. And that a man like me must lack any token of sentiment for anyone or anything.

She remains deflated in front of me. To her credit, she tells me to get out, to get out and never come back. She's right. There's no point in talking to me. I'm a man without introspection, taking what I can. A man not worth screaming at. A man worth nothing.

As she slams the door behind me, I think, at least, I had her. After all that teasing and playing around, I finally possessed her. I prevailed, could think of myself as dominant and victorious. I feel embarrassed, or something close to that, but more for the awkwardness at the door than anything else. In the street, in front of a crowded and locally famous Italian Bakery, I pass a homeless man, red fingers, opaque eyes, crusted, black scabbed calves above his shoes, singing.

"I'll overcome some day…"

A civil rights song, one this White alcoholic has no business singing.

"I'll overcome some day…"

I stop a few feet away. He doesn't care to notice, caught up in his own revelry. He seems to have been frozen decades ago when civil rights marchers and folk singers and hippies took the national stage. He's wearing an Army patch, and I imagine he served a tour in Korea or Vietnam and then spent the rest of his drinking life wondering why. It's too damn cold but he keeps singing:

"This world is one great battlefield,

With forces all arrayed;

If in my heart I do not yield,

I'll overcome some day…"

His skin is flaky and chapped, his hair flecked with dandruff, and he's pissing me off. He's not a Black man, so why is he singing this song? The ground stinks of urine, and there's a bottle in a brown paper bag at his feet. He's the least of my brothers, the ravaged meek who might one day inherit the earth if he manages to get inside before he finishes that bottle, if he isn't dead before the night is out. But he won't stop singing, burdened with a truth that must be revealed: we have to choose sides. That we can be on the side of the smirking men or the side that chooses to overcome them, and that is all. That is our only decision.

He's accusing me in the snow-covered street, that's what he's doing. I'd not sent him and four hundred thousand others to be maimed and killed in another land; I'd not slain the million others. I'd never stabbed or tortured or raped. I'd not hunted Indians, sold slaves, crusaded against infidels, starved Irish, corralled Jews or firebombed cities. I'd not, but this is what the homeless man knows – and there is the entirety of hell in this – I could have.

In a sudden wave of introspection and self-examination, I realize that I am incapable of anything that is not in my own interest. It's as simple and nasty and cowardly as that. God has no plan for me, or if He did, I'd rejected it. In the beginning and the end, it came down to selfishness, nothing more than an impulsive and animal grabbiness. I want and stand apart – above – beyond Mary and Steve and Francesca and everyone else.

"My mind is not to do the wrong,

But walk the narrow way;

I'm praying as I journey on,

To overcome some day."

I think back to Mary, immaculate Mary standing in a white bra and blue panties on the shag carpet, when I first encountered the smirking man I'd become. I wonder if I'd actually made a decision then, or if there'd been no decision to be made. If I'd merely become who I was to be. I'd stood apart – above – beyond, even then. I wonder if there is any other part of me left, the part that existed before Mary, the part that should've held on to Mary like a lifeline, who should've kissed away that tiny laugh line all the days with a teary-eyed and undying gratitude. I fall to my knees in the cold snow. The homeless man notices me for the first time just as, worthless, faithless, I begin: "Our Father, who art in heaven…"

I was roused from my reverie at the front door of the taverna by the sight of Papakakis, breathing heavily and sweating as he meandered down a pathway in the village. I started toward him. He turned away, eyes down as he tried to pass me, exposing a head of greasy hair.

"We need to talk," I said in Greek.

"There is nothing to say."

I was a few feet behind him. "I want her out of jail."

"She is staying in jail."

"You can let her out until the trial. She's not going to leave the island."

"In jail, she must wait."

I stood in his path. As he tried to step to the side, I said, "I can pay."

He stopped and stared down at me without changing the angle of his head. I found myself looking past the dark holes of the fat man's nostrils to his dark baggy eyes. He stuffed his hands into his pockets, sniffed and, just like that, it'd become a matter of negotiation.

"How much?" he asked.

"How much does a boat cost?" It seemed as good a way as any to arrive at a figure.

He swallowed, ran his hand through his hair. "I do not like this woman."

"If she goes to trial in Athens, and they ask her why she did it, she will start talking about the nets. You don't want that."

Papakakis frowned and started walking again, but I knew he was thinking over an amount. After a few steps, he turned and scratched his unshaven chin. "It would take a large amount of money." He ran his hands over, but not through, his slick hair. "I must be buying five new fishing boats and food, other things also."

"How much?"

Papakakis huffed and did some arithmetic on his stubby fingers. "Nine million drachmas," he said.

I quickly did the conversion in my head. With large sums of money, I still had to convert to dollars to comprehend the amount. It was over thirty thousand dollars, much more than I'd imagined, but I didn't have the time to consider it now.

"So you won't send the paperwork to Athens?"

He smiled. "You will lose, you know. You, this woman, Giannopoulos, all of those stupid fishermen, are on the wrong side. You can't stop history. You can't stop progress. It's a new world even here, and all you can do is go along."

"Will you do the paperwork or not? That's all I care about."

"I will be giving you time to get the money."

13

I did have some money tucked away, a cash hangover from
my firehouse days of about twenty-five thousand dollars.
Not the amount that Papakakis wanted but, I was certain,
more than he could refuse. Before I left Boston, it'd crossed
my mind to offer the money anonymously to Francesca – but
that seemed an insult more than anything else, and she would,
of course, be receiving Steve's benefits and pension. I also
considered finding a charity for the money, maybe for lost
firefighters. I did find one, but in the end did nothing. I kept
it for myself, my selfishness intact – this time disguised as a
safety net, should I ever return from my penance of travels.

I'd like to say that my only thoughts were for Kerryn's
welfare and that I withdrew the money immediately. But I
remained captive of my instincts for self-preservation, and my
mind revolted at the prospect of handing over such an amount
of money. If I gave this money away, I'd be cutting the final
connection I had to the outside world, discarding the only
security I possessed. My days of carefree traveling would be
over. I wouldn't have enough for a plane ticket out of Greece
and I'd be stuck. So it seemed I had to decide whether I'd
commit to this island indefinitely, commit to a humble life
in a place I hardly knew and where I had few friends. There

were other countries I wanted to visit, other ferries, and other seas, but the more I thought about leaving, the more I knew I could never go.

I went to the taverna, exchanged some paper currency for a pocket full of change, and walked down the dusty road to a public phone. I poured a handful of coins into the slot and put through the call. The phone, an artifact from another civilization, felt strange in my hand, and I dialed this forgotten instrument awkwardly.

Boston was seven hours behind Greece, but my banker, who served firefighters almost exclusively, was in his office. I remembered him as a tall, cocksure man of about my age, a bit too forward and friendly. He never failed to suggest that we '*grab some brewskis*' whenever I saw him, and I could never tell if the offer was genuine or in some way patronizing. Now, as he answered the phone, he said, yes, of course he remembered me, though I wasn't sure if that were true. He asked how I was getting along. I responded as he would have expected me to and then told him I needed to close my account, and wanted all my money transferred to a bank on the island.

"Really?" his voice registered alarm, but he recovered quickly. "Good for you. I wouldn't come home either if I were there. I've heard about the sun and wine and topless beaches. Must be paradise."

In the way he spoke, there was the underlying assumption that we understood one another; we were both a certain sort of man after all and wanted the same things out of life: pretty women, fast cars, good liquor and a big house for entertaining. I could imagine him winking at me from the other end of the phone, and this infuriated me. It was true, I may have been a man like that once, but I was far from that now. I brought him back to the issue at hand. He said he would work it out but needed me to verify some information.

For a few long moments, I couldn't recall my former address or social security number. I'd forgotten all about them. I no longer had a phone or a license or any sort of account anywhere. Except for the taverna's bankbook, I rarely saw a number. I recalled how reliant that distant continent was on numbers, on the quantification and summing up of almost everything. I was relieved to be done with it, if only for the time being.

When I hung up the phone, I felt agitated, like I had to shake off this man from the other side of the world. I speculated about what he'd think if I'd walked into the bank to make this transaction, if he could see me the way I looked now: unshaven, unkempt, perhaps even depraved. And if I told him that I'd come to the island not for the sun or wine or topless women, but for redemption, what would he have thought? As far as he knew, I was still the hero firefighter.

I believed in redemption, if nothing else. My Catholic education had injected the requisite amount of guilt, it was true, but along with that, the promise of a precise and equal measure of offsetting grace. Like Paul on the road to Damascus, I trusted that, with will and purpose, I could transform my life. The nuns had succeeded in implanting that – and, what's more, they'd given me the framework as well. Like any saint or heretic, I knew I'd have to go to the mountains or desert to develop the moral consciousness I'd forsaken – if, in fact, I ever had one. I'd have to give up all I'd know, quit the Fire Department and quit Boston, quit everyone, including and most importantly myself, if possible. One way or another, I'd have to renounce everything I was and everything I had. I hadn't done that initially. I'd tried to trick the process by leaving some money behind. The fact that I hadn't realized that I was doing that until this moment was irrelevant. Because now I saw, quite clearly, how I'd been respectively pushed, tempted, and pulled into forsaking it all, and that with my mounting involvement with Kerryn and Yukon and the politics of the Reserve, I'd been offered the rare and genuine opportunity to remake myself.

The next time I took the taverna receipts to the bank, the banker Savvas informed me that a large sum of money had arrived for me from America. He regarded me suspiciously, as if this sudden influx of capital confirmed my status as a CIA agent.

I found Papakakis inside his own taverna, and he followed me to the bank in silence. I hesitated before making the transfer to Papakakis' account. It was a risk – there were no documents or signatures or handshakes. Everything was understood without words or witnesses, and this worried me. Of course, Savvas would be witness to the transaction, whatever that was worth. I didn't know what side he was really on, if any, and I'd never seen him in either taverna. I recalled him once mentioning that he believed all bankers should be neutral like Switzerland. If that were the case I'd be able to count on him, despite his suspicions. I breathed out and told Savvas to transfer all the money into Papakakis' account. Moments later, Papakakis and I stood together outside the bank.

I demanded he release Kerryn instantly.

"After," he said.

"After what?' I responded, but he was already on his way to his taverna.

I was furious and started back to the bank to see if I could recover my money. I was almost inside when I understood that Papakakis couldn't release Kerryn until he told the fishermen they'd be getting new boats. There was a certain procedure to be followed, and Papakakis was sure to do that in order to get all the credit coming to him.

Meanwhile, I tried to come to terms with the change I'd just made in my life. I was without money or prospects, no longer the carefree, careless sojourner. Having given everything away, I was now a poor bartender on a poor island, and nothing else.

I watched the soccer game to pass the time. As if to validate my point, Pavlos was paying a price of his own. He was standing in his spot on the side of the field when the ball rolled right past him. He extended his foot to stop it but too late; the ball was already five feet behind him. When the others saw this bungled effort, they laughed and threw clumps of grass and dirt at him.

"Leave," the kids yelled. They were all in it now. "Get out of here. Idiot! Sucker! Loser!"

He turned his back on them, as they continued to pelt him with anything they could pick up. He squatted down on his thighs to make himself as small as possible, and that's when he noticed me standing by the door of the taverna. His head stayed bowed as his eyes rose to meet mine. If only to save him from injury, I waved him over. He ran and was out of breath by the time he made it to the door. As I led him inside, he started to cry.

"A screw-up?" I said, trying to sound upbeat.

"Shaken not poured, he said. He gathered himself as he watched me make his drink. "You go home to Americky soon?" he said.

"Not for a long time."

"But do you think in Americky, the children are mean to me also?"

There was something about Pavlos – a certain naiveté and neediness, an inherent pitiable quality – that would be picked up by kids anywhere. The young in any nation can ferret out the physically and socially inept as easily as kicking a can. So probably nothing would change with Pavlos, no matter where he found himself, but he didn't need to know that.

"Maybe not," I said.

"You take me with you to Americky? I see on map. I draw many things there I see on TV. It is very big, yes?"

"Yes."

"And the houses, so big. Very big, yes?"

"Well, it depends-"

"Yes, but everyone has much space, yes?" he asked scuffing the bottom of his shoes.

"There are all sorts of places. Not everybody –"

"– But everyone has space. So much space. Everyone has so much space." The question became more of a demand. I looked into his upturned eyes.

"Yes," I said finally, unwilling to extinguish his hope. "Everyone has space. A lot of space." I handed him the screw-up and picked a piece of brown grass out of his hair.

He cast a faraway look out the door and stopped shuffling his feet. "With so much space there, I do not know why you come here." He couldn't prevent a smile from rising to his lips. I nodded, acknowledging that he had a point.

I looked out the taverna door to see if anything had yet happened with Kerryn as Pavlos sipped his drink. As I started to straighten the bottles behind the bar, he rested his chin on the wooden edge. He took a thick pencil from his pocket and started looking up and down the bar. There were no napkins so I put a scrap of paper next to him. As before, he kept his chin glued to the bar and began to draw.

"You live near the water," he said. "In the... how you say?" As he talked only the top half of his head lifted, as if on a fulcrum, the bottom half remaining firmly secured.

"Cove."

In time, Pavlos finished his drawing, rose from the stool and headed toward the door. His shirt and shorts were splattered with mud. I looked at the picture. He'd drawn a diminutive fishing boat tossing in an immense wave – a wave so large that it threatened not only the boat but most of the earth and sky as well. It was reminiscent of his other drawing, and I came to the conclusion that Pavlos had, if not a unique talent, at least a unique way of picturing his tiny world.

He stopped at the door. In the harbor behind him, the fishing boats had begun to return.

"You can be my friend?" he asked.

I smiled. "Sure."

"This is for you," he said, pointing to the paper, "In the whole world, it is the only thing I can do. The only thing."

Once again, I discarded the paper without a second thought, as I nervously and impatiently awaited Kerryn's release.

14

I missed it when it actually happened.

Just over an hour later, I stuck my head out the taverna door, and there was Kerryn standing across the dusty road, smiling and holding Bobby wrapped in the green blanket like a baby. As she waved, a sense of relief flooded over me. Papakakis had actually done it; he'd been honorable.

"Hurry home," she called.

The taverna was silent when I returned. Every eye followed me as I walked to the bar. They'd all seen Kerryn free, had heard her urge me home. Now, as I stood wiping down the bar, they were muttering below the level of my hearing. I could imagine what they were saying: that I was a traitor to the taverna, that I was too involved with the fish-woman, that I was CIA.

I debated trying to explain to them why Kerryn would never do anything to their own boats, and that she was only trying to stop the illegal netting. I went so far as to compose the Greek sentences in my head. But when I looked out the door and saw the masts of the boats in the harbor, steady as church steeples, I knew it wouldn't do any good. There was a sanctity about all the boats – no matter what side they were on – a sanctity which Kerryn, an outsider, had desecrated. To them, there could be no defense for her actions.

I kept myself busy behind the bar, counting and re-counting the money in the shoebox, straightening the bottles and cleaning the glasses. In all that time, not a single man ordered a drink and, one by one, they slowly departed. By dinnertime, there was nobody left in the place, and I was just about to close up when Martin arrived. Bobby was stuffed into the pocket of his army jacket, his head stuck out as if riding in a sidecar.

"Woman free and dog returned," he said. "That was all so quick, I'm startin' to think you're a covert agent."

He sat at the bar in the same seat Pavlos had sat in earlier and sipped a beer. I stood across the bar and drank one myself.

"I paid Papakakis," I said.

"How much?" When I told him, he said, "Too much. Should've asked me."

"He wanted to pay for food for the families in the meantime."

"Sure, sure, he'll give away enough to make it look grand and then buy some property near the port. Giannopoulos is going to be pissed-off."

"Where is he?"

"Went to get a loan in Athens. Needs more money to pay the fishermen. Could've used some of yours. You heard about him givin' them money from the fund to help them survive until the election?" I nodded. "Here's a little secret. No fund. Ran out years ago. Giannopoulos is in debt and deep. I told him not to be botherin' with this election, but he couldn't stop himself. 'Course, you really screwed him over, if you gave Papakakis that much money…"

"It was the only way."

"Made Papakakis a hero, is what you did. Imagine what they're sayin' up there." He pointed through the taverna wall toward the village. "Papakakis is probably walkin' around, talkin' about how he took the U.S. government." He looked down at Bobby and said to me, "give us a glass, would you?"

I handed Martin one of the glasses that I'd spent half the day cleaning, and he poured some beer into it. He gently pulled Bobby out of his pocket and placed him on the bar. Bobby was scared; his frog eyes grew even wider. He spread his spindly legs as wide as possible to steady himself. He didn't like being up so high. Martin moved the glass of beer in front of his nose. Bobby sniffed it and snapped his head away quickly.

"One of the few consolations for livin', beer is," Martin said. "Thinkin' I should let Bobby know it's available as soon as possible."

"A little young," I said.

"Doesn't matter. Not like he'll ever have anythin' to do. Won't be seekin' gainful employment in the near future."

After a while Bobby grew bored with the beer and carefully collapsed by gradually spreading his legs apart, inch by inch, until his stomach hit the bar. Martin watched this with amusement, then scooped him up and placed him back into his pocket. Martin chugged the rest of the beer from Bobby's glass.

"May have to fire you," he said.

"For what?"

"Consortin' with the enemy. 'Course it all depends on how the fishermen and Giannopoulos feel about it. I'll do what I can, talk to your bankrupt candidate, but if I were you, I'd be gettin' to work on that CV."

I walked home from the taverna, watching the stars and planets as they appeared, singly, then in multitudes, then in countless numbers. As I broke through the tunnel of trees to the cove I could hear, over the crickets, the gentle sound of the sea lapping against the shore. I strolled into the cove slowly, feeling the dust beneath my feet, the slightly musty odor of stationary water. It all seemed new again, perhaps because everything else had been lost; the sights, sounds and smells of this disregarded place was all I had left – as much a home as anywhere.

Kerryn was lying on the dock when I arrived, staring straight up. When she heard me, she popped up and greeted me with a hug. She held her naked body firmly against mine and squeezed hard with both arms. This sudden, unimpeded intimacy was accompanied by an unsettling sensation, an odd mix of desire and bewilderment, which I held off as best I could.

"Let's go," she said, leaping into the sea.

I stripped and splashed in right behind her. She slapped on the water and whistled; Yukon arrived almost instantly. Holding elbows, we wrapped our arms in front of Yukon's pectoral fins as we shot straight out of the cove and into the middle of the wide Aegean.

As before, Yukon looped up and down, in and out of the water. Only this time there were two of us. Once or twice, I turned to see Kerryn's face: mouth slightly open, neck rigid, eyes lifted upward, racing forward.

When Yukon stopped, there was nothing but sea and sky around us, a sheer blackness punctuated only by the whites of six eyes. I lied on my back to rest and felt the sea hoist me toward the dome of sky. I blinked, and the darkness covered me like a weightless blanket. Yukon, next to me, chirped and squeaked with reckless abandon. I wondered how I could be alone in the open sea, unprotected, naked, in the deepest part of the night, and yet feel so safe, so secure?

Kerryn spun in the water and came toward me, her eyes glued on mine. She wrapped her arms and legs around me. She kissed me and slowly, gently glided one hand down to take me inside her. Instinctively, I pulled away. We sank in the warm water and fell apart.

Kerryn came up smiling, eyes wide. She hadn't realized what I'd done. Yukon emitted her particular chirp-laugh and swam right behind Kerryn, so she was wedged between Yukon and me. Kerryn tried again, this time using Yukon as a backboard. Her breath was warm on my shoulder; her stomach, flat against mine, was wet and slick; her legs pulled me closer and closer. I found myself aware of my own thoughts, aware of the shadow consciousness within me that had first made itself known in Mary's bedroom. And I felt myself pulling away, growing distant, even in the midst of the sea. I wasn't sure how much of me was still the smirking man. It was possible that I still viewed sex as an act of possession and domination, and, especially with Kerryn, that was something I couldn't risk. I kissed her on the nose and gently pushed her way. She didn't seem to mind, and with a squeeze of my hand, we wrapped arms around Yukon and soared back to the cove.

Later as we rested on the dock, I felt the need to explain. "Maybe there're some things you should know, some things that –"

She placed a gentle finger on my mouth. "No. Forget it. Do what I do," she said. She put her arms under her waist, rose up, lifted her legs and pointed her toes at the bold, gray moon resting lazily in the sky. "Aim your sight between your feet. Find a beam of light from the moon and try to feel it pulling you. Concentrate. The moon is a benevolent master, the guardian angel of the night. Yearn to be drawn to its luster."

She let her legs fall back down to the dock and raised her arms. I did the same.

"If oceans follow the moon, ebbing and flowing according to its pull, then why can't we? What keeps us so firmly rooted to the earth?" She brought her hands down and kicked her legs flat out on the dock. Again, I followed.

"Feel the pull, so subtle at this distance, lifting you up, up, up. Concentrate on the pull. Don't think about anything else. It'll only weigh you down."

I stared at a small, beetle-shaped shadow on the face of the moon. I didn't feel any pull from the moon, not yet anyway. I tried to empty myself of tedious thoughts.

"See how the moon rests so solidly, pulling at the oceans. If you stare at it long enough, you can almost feel time itself becomes suspended, until you don't think, don't feel, but are just aware." She lowered her voice to a whisper, "Radiant light and warmth, the sea lapping against the dock, crickets chirping, a graceful breeze. Is there any room for worries in that? Any past or future?"

She stretched her hands and feet, struggling to extend them as far as they could go. "There are two worlds. There is this world – the here and now... In this cove, this world, you are an indistinct part of all that surrounds you, no less and no greater than the trees, the ants, the sea, the crickets, the fish, the sky. That's what the moon and the cosmos are trying to tell you. That other world – the world outside – that doesn't exist. That's a place where being demands justification, a world of pasts and futures, of domination and submission, of misinterpretations. Don't you see how you are diminished there?"

She pointed her toes again and reached for her ankles. In that position, she rocked back and forth, as if trying to lift herself off the dock.

"Try it," she said, and I did, grabbing my ankles and rocking. "See how one part of your back remains planted. One part keeps you grounded. Any part of you planted in the other world is the part that's holding you down. When all you have to do here is be, just be. If you let go of what holds you down, you can float; you can fly. Isn't that what the moon is telling us? Floating and flying are only a matter of letting go, merely a case of casting off weight, the past, the future, all possessions, reducing drag."

There was a quick, familiar sound in the water below us and, as if from nowhere, a splash announced Yukon's return. The spray flew up and arched back down over the dock, obscuring my view of the moon. I was under a shower now, a thousand drops descending back toward earth. I waited, tensing, closing my eyes, suspending time, being right here, right now, free for an instant, a harmony of flesh, consciousness and soul...

And then it came, water raining down, cool beats of exhilaration all over my body.

15

I'd walked halfway to the village, when I heard the intermittent, squeaky sounds of Harry and Ari's Fiat from behind me. They stopped and asked me if I wanted a ride, saying they'd been on the other side of the island checking on their tomato plants. I jumped into the back as before, wedging my knees against the front seat. They drove and shifted as they always did, Ari manipulating the pedals, Harry shifting gears. *"En-ah... thee-oh... thee-oh... THEE-OH!"*

I watched the brown road speed beneath the holes in the floorboard as Harry grinded the gears into place. When, at last, we were cruising securely in third gear, Harry called out, rather loudly, *"Pro-so-hee."* At first, I thought he was speaking to Ari. *Pro-so-hee* means 'attention' or 'watch out', so I concluded that Harry was talking about something on the road. But then Ari repeated the word – *"pro-so-hee"* – and stared at me in the rear view mirror.

This time I asked outright if they were speaking to me. Harry said 'yes', and then, with an uncharacteristically heavy tone, told me that they'd had heard rumors that Papakakis, now that he had his money, was going to take revenge against 'the fish-woman' and possibly myself as well. Papakakis wants to teach us a lesson, Ari added, though no one knows what that lesson might be. As my friends, they said they wanted to warn me but didn't want anyone at the taverna to see them talking to me. When I started to ask questions, they simply reiterated their admonition to be careful and dropped me off just before the village, before anyone could see that I'd been riding with them.

As soon as I opened up the taverna, Giannopoulos came in and sat at a table near the door. It was the first time I had seen him since I gave Papakakis the money. I put a large pitcher of retsina and a glass on his table.

"On me," I said.

"Generous with everyone these days, aren't you? I get retsina, and Papakakis gets the whole island."

"That wasn't my intention."

"See that harbor? The simple boats? The clear blue sea? Take a close look, because it will never be the same."

"I had to help her."

"What's the worst that could have happened? She goes to Athens, they ask her to pay something and leave the country. She goes back to where she came from. It's not the worst thing. You could go with her."

"But the dolphin would —"

"*Panaigitsa mu!* Enough of this stupid dolphin." He took a sip of retsina directly from the pitcher and wiped his mouth with the sleeve of his white polo shirt. "Sometimes, you have to think about other than yourself or some stupid dolphin. I know this is not your home, but it was my father's home, and it is the home of these men." He made a broad sweep of his arm. "Sometimes you must do what is right, no matter the cost."

"The dolphin is part of what's saving this island. The existence of the dolphin is part of what makes the Reserve worthwhile. Get rid of the dolphin, and there's one less thing to preserve."

"You're wrong. Dolphins come and go. They always have. Just as you will come and go, and I will, and every other person who lives here. We're not trying to preserve ourselves but preserve a way of living. We may be the last ones." He turned his back to me and looked toward the sea, but continued talking. "For five thousand years, the men here fished, and this island remained the same like it always was. But you have done your part to put an end to that. Maybe I didn't have much of a chance at winning this election, okay, but I had something… the hope of a chance. But you have removed that. I will still try to win the election. It's all I know how to do. But you've taken part in killing everything here, and I wish you had never come. Now leave me alone."

I rose from his table and walked back to the bar saddened by how it came to be that people on the island who all wanted the same thing could end up damaging each other in so many different ways. Subsequently, I spent the day in a melancholy mood, serving the fishermen silently and deftly avoiding Giannopoulos' eyes, as he avoided mine.

The melancholy disappeared when I arrived back at the cove in the darkening night and encountered once again the black glass of sea and a tickling warm breeze carrying a chorus of crickets. There was a candle lit in Kerryn's shack, the mild glow wavering unsteadily into the cove through the open door. She was in bed when I entered. Wordlessly, I climbed in next to her.

"Pavlos saw me with Yukon." She wasn't happy about it.

"Pavlos came here? He's never been here before."

"He said he wanted to make a painting of the cove. To thank you. For the drinks you've been giving him." She raised her eyes to mine.

"Non-alcoholic."

"Right. I had to scare him. It was all I could think of. Imagine if word ever got out back to Papakakis about Yukon. He doesn't know she's in the cove every day. At least I don't think he does. Would he have let me out so easily if he knew that? I told Pavlos if he ever told anyone, I wouldn't be his friend and neither would you. Things are bad enough."

I said nothing. Perhaps it was best she believed it all had happened that way – that Papakakis had just let her out *so easily*. She would find out that I paid Papakakis soon enough. Everyone knew everything on the island, and even though Kerryn was removed from the gossip, it was impossible to believe she wouldn't find out one way or another. There would be plenty of time for that later, however, and I left her to her own thoughts. We went to sleep in each other's arms.

In the middle of the night, I woke to find Kerryn sneaking out of the shack. After I heard the splash in the water, I rose and cracked open the door. Yukon was already in the cove, and Kerryn mounted her with an aggressive, forthright manner. And Kerryn's body, so tame in the bed next to me, grew wild and loose clasped around Yukon. It was as if the night had created a hunger within her, a hunger satiated only by Yukon. I watched as their bare bodies, clenched together, tipped, looped and propelled their way out to sea in a rhythmic rocking of woman and beast, until the night swallowed them.

As the note of a thousand crickets droned on, I remained in the doorway thinking that life may be no more than a celebration of difference, difference in anatomies, in sensations and perception, and that perhaps, just perhaps, the greater the discrepancies fused the greater the possibilities. It was about connecting to something beyond yourself, extending your embrace to take in as much as possible – that was the greater plan for all of us, and, within that, as much meaning and validation as I could ever hope to find.

I feigned sleep when Kerryn returned to the bed, still damp. As she dozed off next to me, I felt a certain soulfulness in the darkness, naked on the hard bed, and discovered I'd made a mistake. I'd been seeking grace like an object to be found, a place to be discovered. But I now understood that grace can't be earned, nor is it bestowed on desperate pilgrims like manna from heaven. It isn't that difficult. Grace is our birthright, there in the warmth of the sun, the blue of the sky and dirt beneath our feet, in every heartbeat.

I turned over and took in the sea-logged smell of Kerryn's skin, the slow widening curve of her waist, the sloping indent of her stomach. I ran the back of my finger against her arm, and she awoke.

Her eyes looking upward grew damp. She turned those damp eyes to me and a glance, soft as a cloud, lay between us. She spoke lightly, sensitively, as if she feared that soft cloud might blow away: "It's lonely here sometimes."

"I imagine."

"At times, I find myself dreaming of being in a group, a community, like those people in the States, the ones that live without electricity or modern things –"

"The Amish?"

"The Amish, right. What I've heard is that when their kids get to a certain age, they send them out into the modern world to see what it's like. The kids can decide to stay there or return back. And most of them do, most return. I think about a community where people and families live in with almost nothing but the earth, the sea and each other. Take what's given; do no harm; all that. And any kids there, at a certain age, they can go out into the world, see what it's like, and return if they want. I think they would return, most of them, and maybe bring others with them. People who are tired of competition and getting and spending and modern living. And these new people could have children and do the same with them, send them out to see if they return. That way whole islands could be populated, first one, then another, then maybe another."

The emotions came through again, this time in her eyes, which widened as she hurried through the last words. I wasn't sure if she was longing for the family she'd never had in this scenario, or if that were too simple an explanation.

"I may sound like an idealist or a cult freak," she continued, "but I don't think I am... not too much anyway. It would be just a group of people trying to live together and competing, if that's the word, for *less* – less things and less harm and less cruelty and more of everything that can't be measured. That would be the striving. It's a crazy idea, I know, but... but it could start with a single man and woman. And the truth is, maybe it would end there. With just two people on an island. But even then, it's nice to think about. Don't you think it's nice to think about?"

"I do."

"Right," she said. Then she closed her eyes and returned to sleep without another thought.

Far away the mountain and its attendant fires loomed high and bright but ever remote. With those words, I trusted, foolishly, that those fires would never touch us.

16

I woke with a lightness, a giddiness that seemed an entirely new way of greeting the day. Kerryn paraded naked in front of me – doe-eyed, wiry, bronzed – pasting a big '62' on the wall. In a small pile in the middle of the shack were more things she was tossing away: pens and underwear, a pot, a calculator, as well as some letters. She didn't need any of these things. She wore few, if any, clothes, no shoes, no jewelry, no make-up.

I lay on the bed and counted her possessions as she proceeded through her waking ritual: she woke up (5 items – bed frame, mattress, pillow, two sheets), soaped her face and dried it (3 items – soap, towel, bottle of water), brushed her teeth (2 – toothbrush, tooth paste), combed her hair (1 – comb), had a cup of coffee (3 – the coffee itself, spoon, cup), ate a piece of fruit (1 – banana) and put on her morning clothes (2 – shorts and tee shirt only, no underwear). These things alone totaled 17 items, more than one quarter of her total.

She told me her desire was to get to less than 20 items. That morning, for fun, I tried to make her count bananas in a different way, arguing that the four bananas together were actually one bunch. She told me that I still looked at getting rid of things as a difficulty. Of course, I never inquired why the four bananas counted as four objects but a few hundred sheets of paper counted as one. Marshmallows, I'd discovered, were not counted at all. There was a bag in the kitchen. She loved marshmallows, she told me with a grin, and tried to keep a few on hand for special occasions.

Suddenly, there was a sound outside, an unusual, human sound. Kerryn heard it too.

"Wait here," I said.

I pulled on some shorts and opened the door expecting to see Papakakis or one of his fishermen. Instead, I saw Pavlos standing on the dock, throwing a ball to Yukon, who batted it with her nose right back at him. More often than not, Pavlos dropped it.

For the next half-hour or so, while I prepared for work, Pavlos played with Yukon. When I was ready to go, I called for him to leave with me. But he declined, and I couldn't convince him otherwise. I looked back to Kerryn and shrugged by way of apologizing for my helplessness. We both knew that, somehow, his presence in the cove would become a problem.

Before I reached the tunnel of trees I noticed, traced in the sand and dirt, a depiction of the island. As usual, the proportions had been distorted – the mountain, gigantic in stature, rose far above the clouds, dominating the sea and sky. And nothing else seemed to matter; the houses and boats were negligible, the people too small to be seen.

I turned back to Pavlos, just in time to see him clumsily drop the ball that Yukon had batted back to him. He was an instinctive artist, Pavlos, drawing his chimerical empires almost unconsciously, whenever and wherever he could. I couldn't help but wonder if there was a place for artists like Pavlos or unencumbered beings like Kerryn or gentle creatures like Yukon on an island such as this. I wondered if there was a place for them, or for myself, anywhere.

"Word on the dark side of the harbor is you're *filotimos*," Martin told me at the taverna. He'd been the first to arrive. He put Bobby on the ground, who quickly spun in a tight full circle, lied down, and was asleep by the time that Martin placed his hat on top of him. "No one can believe you actually paid nine million drachmas."

"I don't know this word, *filotimos*."

"A good one. *Filo* means 'friend' and *timo* means 'honor' so the word means 'friend of honor.' High praise and better than what they call me."

"Which is?"

"*Filo-beera*." Martin's hat slid a few inches as Bobby rearranged himself. "So when will you and Kerryn be goin' away?"

"What do you mean?"

"Weren't you warned?"

"Not by Papakakis."

"If he sniffed that much money, he wasn't goin' to risk losing it." He shrugged again. "But he can't let you stay. It'd be humiliatin' for him to have you around. People might eventually find out how much you paid him and he can't have that."

Martin took the hat off Bobby, flipped it over and then scooped him inside. The dog barely flinched and went back to sleep immediately.

"I have no intention of leaving, just when —" I stopped myself.

Martin stared at me for a long moment. "Then you better watch out," he said eventually. "You'd better watch out."

❧

When I reached the cove that night, neither Kerryn nor Yukon was there. I was disappointed, having hoped for another night with them. Eventually, I lay down on the dock and stared at the pale moon, rising in the sky. For a time, I tried to feel its pull, tried again to let go of all that held me down. But I was very tired and fell asleep. Hours later, Kerryn woke me up. It was now a starless, moon-bright night. The sea and sky stretched out infinitely, and the heat that had not yet squandered itself surrounded us. She squeezed my hand.

"You'll be the first person to see this," she whispered.

She grabbed the red towel from the steps and threw it in the water, then pushed me in after it. She began to call Yukon from the steps, whistling and slapping. Shortly after, there was the signature ripping sound at the edge of the cove, and Yukon arrived. We jumped in together. Kerryn put the red towel in Yukon's mouth and held on to one end. I grabbed the other end so we were on opposite sides of the dolphin as she pulled away.

I felt the immense propulsion generated by Yukon's fluke with each thrust. It seemed as if Yukon was in a hurry; we gained speed rapidly. My hands strained to maintain a grip on the red towel while the water tugged fiercely at my shoulders and legs. In an instant, the cove was gone, and we were in the open sea. I glanced at Kerryn. She had her head cocked up and forward, her eyes squinted in determination.

I closed my eyes and ducked my head under the surface. The *whoosh* of the water was gone, transformed into a sort of muted hum. Fighting the pull of the water, I snapped my head back above the surface. I tried to gauge our speed, but there was nothing to measure it against. We were a rocket in space, tearing from one void to another, only the salt shooting up my nose and down my throat made me aware of the distance being covered.

We must have turned at some time because I could now see the island over my right shoulder. Again, Kerryn and I were helpless and naked and exposed and entirely in Yukon's element. Yukon could take us anywhere; she could pull us under or strand us or crash us into a rock. But my momentary fear was of no consequence; like a child leaping into the open arms of his father, the apprehension and delight sprang from the same source, one was impossible without the other. Yukon was pulling us into the night, and we could only abandon ourselves to her will.

Whether we made another turn or not, I wasn't sure, but soon we were heading back into the island. It was a part of the island I had not seen before. There were sheer falling cliffs of white rock, descending into the sea. The sea had cut thousands of large and small holes into the rocks, forming mysterious hollows and dugouts.

We slowed and penetrated an opening in one of the cliffs, beneath a jagged arc of sea-bitten rocks, no more than seven feet across. We entered what appeared to be a giant inverted cone. There was a small beach of white sand about twenty feet wide ahead of us. And above white rocks shot toward the sky, closing into smaller concentric circles as they advanced. There was the tiny opening where we had entered and an opening at the top – that was all.

Kerryn let go of the towel and swam to the shore. I followed her. Yukon was last and slid herself onto the sand, dropping the towel from her mouth and keeping half her body in the water. The moon like a bottle cap hung just above the top opening. The light beamed in, gentle and sweet, funneled down by the rock. On the sides of this funneling rock, tiny prisms of crystal angled the vertical white moonlight into a horizontal tangle of red, blue and yellow colors, a thin rainbow streaking across the moon. The moon itself seemed so close and so small, that I felt I could climb through the tangle of colors across the sky and nudge it.

Kerryn sat with her feet in the water, and Yukon flopped over and rested her nose in Kerryn's lap. Kerryn threw her head back and smiled.

"The sanctuary," Kerryn said, her voice echoing up into the funnel.

I stared at her, and the way the light from above caught the white rim of Kerryn's deep eyes reminded me of the eclipse. Her forehead glistened with sea and sweat, and she sat with her mouth, pink and moist, partly open. On the sand behind me was a half-full bottle of water and a small statue, no bigger than a foot, a burnt gray and white female figurine with a long nose and a rounded cut-off head. To my eye, the ancient statue was without flaws or cracks, as if it existed in a vacuum.

"Cycladic age, I think," she said. "Could be five thousand years old."

"How'd she get here?"

I'd heard there were thousands of sculptures dotting the Aegean floor but few, I was sure, as old or in as good a shape as this one, which could be the prize piece in any museum.

"I don't know. It was here when I first came," she said. "Yukon found this place. One night, after we'd been riding further and further out, she brought me here. This was just before the others left, and that's when I knew I had to stay. I mean, I guess, we had a special connection before that. We'd been riding alone at night. But when she brought me here, I knew, just *knew* that I had to stay."

I looked at Yukon's kind face, the sleek rounded head, the large eyes, the fixed smile, resting in the lap of Kerryn. Yukon shot a sly glance in my direction as if to affirm what

Kerryn was saying. I laughed, moved next to Kerryn and petted the side of Yukon's body. Yukon clicked with glee and I
was reminded of the forts I used to build as a kid, cardboard
and pillows constructed to keep the real world out and the
imaginary one in. The fact that we were naked, like children,
and with an animal, like children, was as if I had somehow
re-claimed a last slice of innocence.

And here it was. In the present. And it was real.

Yukon lying contentedly right next to Kerryn was real,
and the sea was real, and the canopy of rainbow lights was real
and Kerryn, her golden skin glowing in the flue of moonlight,
was real.

"In this place, I began to realize that there was so much
more to Yukon," she said, "so many layers and depths to her
being. It changed my life. I realized that we can't claim a
spiritual or moral existence – we can't claim a soul – unless
we grant the same claim to all other sentient creatures, such as
Yukon. Only a soulful being could know of a place like this."

"It seems so far away, so removed, from everything."

She stroked my thigh, slowly, sensually before answering.
"It's a sanctuary. And this place – like all places could be – is
merely the physical manifestation of the thoughts and desires
of the creatures that inhabit it. That's what I think. Some
animals and some people want love, so there is that, others
want tragedy, so there is suffering, others want fights, so there
are wars, some want to have what others don't, so there is scarcity. We find what we seek. But this place is not part of that
outside world. It's a sanctuary, made up of only the thoughts
and desires of the beings who enter into it – my desires and
Yukon's and now yours. It's timeless. It's like practicing for
eternity."

The water lapped on our feet. Yukon's eyes glowed and
wandered about slowly, taking it all in, as if she could under-

stand. Kerryn's arms were wet on my shoulders, and she was radiant in the reflected light, her deep eyes dark and glistening. I was flooded with gratitude, expectation and desire, and felt I'd reached my destination.

I laughed. "I don't even know why I'm laughing."

She smiled. "I think it's the impression of timelessness. What you're feeling is your soul, the link between you and eternity. Dolphins have an exceptionally strong link to the eternal, much stronger than humans. That's the reason I'm trying to get rid of my possessions. Ego, possessions, all that nonsense, deadens the soul. The Buddha, Jesus, Mohammed, they all said the same thing. Get rid of your stuff. Give it away. It ties you down. See the monks with only a robe and bowl. They are strengthening their souls, reinforcing the link. Look at the dolphins: they have nothing. Look at their laughter, their playfulness, their happiness, the way they live their lives, and you will see evidence of a soul. You will see them living the way we're all supposed to live."

Yukon began a series of sharp clicks followed with a very high pitched squeak. The sounds funneled up above our heads and, it seemed, directly to the moon. Then the echo began, and the sounds descended back, only slightly fainter. Yukon kept clicking and squeaking, until the entire sanctuary was full of clicks and squeaks dashing about in an acoustic wonderland, all at different pitches and volume.

I stared hard at the crossing rainbows of lights against the backdrop of the white moon. And as if lifted by the cascading sounds, I felt myself floating just beneath the reds and greens and yellows of the rainbow. I felt as if I could shoot to the moon and look down at the empty shell of my body on the beach. I leaned in and pulled her close.

Yukon stopped clicking. I stared into Kerryn's face as the sounds echoed away, my reflection shining back in her eyes.

She whispered, "yes," and I rolled on top of her just as a soft breeze lofted into the sanctuary. The breeze seemed to be bearing strange, faraway odors, reminiscent of African princesses and Middle East sheiks, of spices from India and silk from China. Odors of depth and mystery.

As these strange odors entered my body, I entered hers. As I eased inside of this yielding, moist and gasping woman, my heart opened like a wound. For the first time, I let it go, bleeding warmly into every hastening pulse of my vulnerability and desire. Nothing mattered but to inhabit Kerryn, to coast and glide and slide through the healing balm of her body. I wanted to impart these feelings to her, to make them known in some way. But my coarse body, huffing and sweating and thrusting as it covered hers, was an inadequate translator. All I could do was trust that through an alchemy of flesh she absorbed them, as my body became possessed by an untroubled, connected, and enlightened being who mingled seamlessly with the sky above, the woman below and the lapping sea. For a few ephemeral minutes, I was that vessel of thoughtless rapture, one part in a rhapsody of man, woman and nature: breathing, yearning, rocking, struggling to get deeper into the wonder...

Later, when we started to leave, I looked back at the small marble figurine. She was worth a fortune on the mainland; all we had to do was bring her back with us. As Kerryn was preparing to leave, putting the towel in Yukon's mouth, I almost mentioned it. But the proud, perfect Cycladic woman stood in defiance of my intentions, just as she had defied the ravages of nature for five thousand years. She was luminous, almost eternal, perfectly preserved. I didn't need her, I told myself, and so I left her as I'd found her, right where she belonged. It was then that I sensed something tender in the air and, silent within the whisper of the generous earth, something nameless

150

and precious that I'd left behind in childhood and had been looking for ever since.

I entered the water and grabbed one end of the towel in Yukon's mouth. Before we left, Yukon chirped one final time. We waited, motionless, listening as the sound peaked, echoed, softened, and then slowly vanished, journeying to the sky.

17

L ight-headed and exhilarated from the night before, I rolled over and was stabbed by a shaft of sunlight from the open door of the shack. I squinted to see outside. Kerryn wasn't in sight and had apparently forgotten to close the door. The wind was up and stirred the dust that hovered in the sunlight. There was dampness in the air, what I took for the leading edge of autumn, of change. I pulled on my shorts and rose from the bed.

I heard something outside, an unrecognizable sound. I ignored it, figuring it to be the bending of the wind through the trees or the sea on the shore. I took a sip of water and heard it again. This time I recognized it. It was Kerryn, her voice distant and desperate. I bounded out the door and searched the water for splashes or swells or ripples. I looked around so fast I couldn't focus, then forced my eyes to stay steady, searching levelly over the cove. There were ten places she could be, a swirl here, some white water over there, a small rise further out.

Something was wrong, I knew it. Was this what Ari and Harry had warned me about? I glared across the water once more, looking for some sort of sign, then ran onto the dock. I heard her again, somewhere, her voice faint but sharp.

"–ife!" is all I heard.

I spotted her, a black head bobbing near the outer edge of the cove. I was about to jump when she waved me off. She was gesturing so frantically that for a split second I thought she was drowning. But no, she was frenzied but not in danger.

"Don't jump! Stop!"

Her words rifled through the air and struck me like a club. I stood at the end of the dock, staring out, holding my breath.

"GET - THE - KNIFE!" She screamed slowly.

"Why? What –?"

But she was already under the water. I wheeled and sprinted back to her shack. Inside, I searched for a knife, cursing at every empty cabinet, at the bare walls and bare desk – at her preposterous resolve to limit possessions. At last, I found a knife on the desk, the blade slightly longer than my hand. I raced back to the dock.

Kerryn saw me and swam toward the dock. I put the knife in my mouth and dove in toward her. I went as far as I could under water then broke the surface. I stroked and kicked frantically, feeling the knife cutting into the corners of my lips. I met Kerryn midway. Her eyes were wide and fearful. I handed her the knife, blade first, and she clenched her hand around it.

"What is it?" I asked.

"Yukon's in a net," she said, putting the knife in her mouth and turning around, "and –"

She hit the water before she finished.

I watched her take two quick strokes away from me. I wiped my mouth and caught sight of the pinkish blood on my hand. I felt no pain. Kerryn was already swimming away. I followed.

We swam to the edge of the cove as fast as possible. Kerryn was the faster swimmer, and the distance between us increased. In front of me, Kerryn took a deep swallow of air and dived down. A few more strokes, and I did the same. The water was clear and blue. It was a long way down, further than I thought. Kerryn was six feet below me, kicking and pumping to go deeper. I trailed her.

Then I saw it: the net cast like a silent ghost across the sea floor. Caught in it, Yukon and Pavlos struggling wildly, ten feet from one another.

Both sets of eyes were glued to the surface, quivering seductively above. Both were battling to escape, flailing and flipping and tossing in rapid, angular thrusts. But their attempts were in vain. They entangled themselves further with every move. Kerryn looked from one to the other, four terror-filled eyes – dolphin and human – begging for release. Suddenly Yukon went limp in the net. Pavlos continued to struggle.

Kerryn hesitated; she had to choose between them. She looked from one to the other and back again.

She swam to Yukon and began cutting, leaving Pavlos to fend for himself. Seconds passed, more. How many? How long would it take? I tried to reach Pavlos but ran out of breath before I could get there. I rose to the surface.

Kerryn was coming up for breath as I swam down to Pavlos. I tried to grab a hold of his arms, but they were everywhere. Long, long, moments passed before I secured his wrist and began to pull. As I pulled, the net shifted with Pavlos' body. I tugged harder and my grip slipped. I swam to the side, grabbed one of Pavlos' legs and tried to pull him from the net. No use – Pavlos had twisted and flipped himself into a hopeless tangle. I had to breathe. Pavlos had hold of my hand. He was stronger than I could imagine; I couldn't go up. Fear gripped me, a spark of adrenaline and my strength increased. I kicked to free myself, mercilessly, viciously. Pavlos could not keep his grip.

I darted to the surface.

A jumble of thoughts crowded my mind about how to save Pavlos: kick him unconscious and untangle him, pull the whole net up, take the knife from Kerryn and cut him free. This last notion seemed the most reasonable, but I reconsidered the next instant. No, I thought, no, Kerryn knows what she is doing. She is in her element. Perhaps Pavlos can survive longer than Yukon without air. Kerryn knows what she is doing.

Kerryn knows.

Kerryn surfaced next to me, took a deep breath and re-submerged. Again, she headed for Yukon. I went to Pavlos. He'd started to inhale water and now went out of control, arching and curling his back against the stranglehold of the net. Five feet away, Kerryn was quickly and methodically cutting the net from around Yukon. Pavlos lurched back and forth. I glimpsed Pavlos' eyes, glazed and terror-filled. He opened his mouth, a scream or a breath. I couldn't get a firm hold. I turned toward Kerryn.

Yukon was free.

Together Kerryn and Yukon darted to the surface, the cut strands of netting float down next to their bodies. Then Kerryn was next to me. But by this time Pavlos was limp. He had ceased his struggles. I rose. I left him. I needed to breathe.

When I returned, Kerryn had cut the lines from Pavlos' body with the knife. Pavlos' white eyes were wide open, his arms and legs were still. I tugged his body. One leg was free, then another. Finally, the whole body floated away from the net. Kerryn and I grabbed one arm each and pulled Pavlos to the surface.

We floated him on his back. I tried to make him breathe by pounding on his chest. Kerryn assisted, pushing on Pavlos' chest with one hand while supporting his back with the other.

"Breathe, Pavlos, breathe."

We swam as fast as we could to the dock, pulling Pavlos between us. I was the first one on the stairs and dragged Pavlos onto the dock. I tilted Pavlos' head back, opened his mouth, puffed into it in short, abbreviated breaths. I pointed where to push on the chest.

"Five quick breaths, then you push three times, right there." I tapped a spot just below the mid-cage.

She followed my orders. Pavlos' skin was chalky white, and he looked as if he had been inflated. He was still and silent; his unblinking eyes stared at the morning sun. After some time, I knew it wasn't working. I felt powerless.

"I'm going to get help," I yelled and took off in the direction of the village.

Sweating and screaming, I stumbled down the path and then onto the dusty road. I prayed for Ari's car. I ran and told myself I cannot get tired. *I cannot be tired.* My lungs burned. My feet slipped on the dust, lacked traction. I kept moving. It seemed an endless journey until I stood at the edge of the village screaming in Greek and English.

"*Ella!* Help! Please! *Para-kalo!* Help! *Voe-eth-ia! Voe-eth-ia!*"

Some kids ran at me, and I told them to call a doctor and get help. Adults emerged, running down the tiny pathways from their houses.

"Pavlos," I cried. "Pavlos! Pavlos!"

I took off for the cove with three of the kids and two of the adults behind me. Others went for help. The kids overtook me and went on ahead. The adults fell behind. I was running again. I was exhausted, almost debilitated. I couldn't catch my breath but kept my legs moving. My bare feet burned with the constant pounding against the hot road. At last, I burst through the tunnel of trees and saw Kerryn still breathing into Pavlos' mouth, her fingers pinching his nose. Three kids were gathered around.

The two adults arrived. I stood over Kerryn, next to the kids. More people arrived, alone and in clusters. I wondered, oddly, angrily, how many of them had been to the cove before. I wondered how many had even known it existed. We stood around like mutes, watching Kerryn's desperate pushes on Pavlos' chest.

"Please, Pavlos, please," she pleaded with every push of her hands. She'd started to cry.

I looked around again, and there was a crowd. I saw Ari and Harry and Yannis the Red and more of the fishermen from both tavernas in torn shirts and dirty brown pants. They said nothing. No one wanted to stop Kerryn, all of them afraid of what that would mean.

The island doctor arrived, an old, small man. He cut his way through the silent crowd at a brisk pace. He asked someone how long Kerryn had been doing this. No one seemed to know. He looked at me.

"Twenty, thirty minutes," I said. It was a guess. I'd lost all track of time.

He walked over to Kerryn and placed a gentle hand on her shoulder. Kerryn looked up for the first time and squinted into the face of the old man. He had a thin white lining of hair like a halo just above his ears. He nodded to her. I had heard good things about this man, how he once cured Yannis' fever and Harry's foot problems. He bent over Pavlos. It was a controlled motion, not easy, the slow movements of brittle bones. He placed a thick, wrinkled hand on Pavlos' limp wrist and put a veiny ear over his mouth. He tested the skin of the legs and arms. He pushed on the chest. Then he massaged the white halo around his head and rose.

"*Pethanay*," the doctor said and only that.

He is dead.

As if on command, the men began to cross themselves and the ladies began to wail. Children darted away, putting distance between themselves and the body. The sun beat down, white and hot. The women began to cry, moaning *They-ay mu, They-ay mu* – my God, my God – through their tears. There were breathless gasps, incredulous wails and long sighs.

I regarded it all as a spectator. I was numb. Kerryn was still kneeling on the ground, on the soaked planks of the dock, staring at the swollen body of Pavlos.

Pavlos was dead. The thought struck like a slammed door. And quickly, so quickly, I was wishing I could take it all back, all of it, the coming to Greece, my friendship with Pavlos, the taverna, Yukon, Kerryn… take it all back. Did I think I could escape anything by leaving my home, by coming to this island? Why did I ever give Pavlos a drink? Why did he come to the cove? Who laid the net? Why didn't Kerryn save Pavlos first?

I wanted to get away from the noises of the crowd. My strongest impulse, my only impulse, was to be alone.

"But how?" someone demanded of me. "How?"

"Caught in the net." It was all I could manage. The words came out of my mouth, but it was as if someone else had said them; they were disenfranchised sounds, not from me, not from anyone. More questions: Why was he in the net? Whose net? Why was Pavlos here? What was he doing in the cove?

I didn't respond.

Nobody responded.

Kerryn rolled herself into a ball, as if she'd been kicked in the stomach. Nothing was said about Yukon, nothing about the terrible choice made. Pavlos and Yukon, it was too much for me to think about.

The old doctor spotted the red towel on the steps of the dock. He took the towel by two corners and covered Pavlos' face with it. The ends of the towel shivered in the wind, Pavlos' body motionless below it.

I was still standing on the dock as Pavlos' body was carried away by four young men. I recognized three of the kids from the soccer games in which Pavlos never played. Two of them were crying. The old doctor left with the body, and the crowd scattered.

All I wanted was to be alone. I looked at Kerryn, still huddled on the dock. There was nothing I could do for her. I turned and headed back to my shack, saying nothing.

"You all right?" Martin asked behind me.

I hadn't even seen him arrive. He placed a hand on my arm, tapped once and removed it.

I stumbled back to my shack, closed the door behind me and closed all the shutters. The room seemed foreign to me; I had spent so little time here since I started seeing Kerryn. It could be a dark place even in the morning. I lay on the floor and stared at the ceiling, waiting for something – anything – to happen. Though I knew it had already happened, I waited. And so it was hours, many hours until the darkness in my shack was equaled by the darkness of the evening, and the darkness inside and the darkness outside were one and the same.

18

In the afternoon of the next day, I pulled myself together as best I could and made my way to the village without seeing Kerryn. The night before, time had passed in a lagging reality, my mind inescapably fixed on Pavlos' bloated body on the dock, the sun burning holes into his unblinking eyes. And, of course, there were doubts: what could I have done differently? Should I have gotten another knife? Should I have taken the knife from Kerryn? Could I have pulled him away more forcefully?

I resisted placing blame on Kerryn. I cast blame at Papakakis and his fishermen. Then I started in on myself, cursing my ineptness under the water, my poor lung capacity, my lack of resolve. I'd had chances but never saved anyone from anything. None of that mattered now, of course.

The harbor was full of fishing boats when I arrived, and there was a small crowd of fishermen waiting outside our taverna. I opened the door, and they followed me inside. Not a word was spoken as they took their seats. I, too, made as few sounds as possible as I set up, taking extra care not to clink the glasses or rattle the change. It was relatively early for the fishermen, and I figured they'd be drinking coffee so I boiled some water. It was Harry who spoke first.

"The fish-woman," he said. "She did the best she could."

When the rest of the fishermen nodded or grunted in agreement, I turned my back so they couldn't see my stunned expression. It simply hadn't occurred to me that they could view Kerryn favorably, but now I realized that they knew nothing of the decision Kerryn had made. How could they? They only knew that she had pulled Pavlos from the net and tried to resuscitate him.

"*Ena café,*" a fisherman called out behind me. I turned around to face them. A number of fishermen raised a hand or finger ordering for themselves. I fixed the coffees and made my way among the tables, placing them as the fishermen motioned to me. When I came to Ari's table, he placed his hand on my arm. "The nets were from Papakakis," he said. "Not supposed to be close to land. They have been removed and destroyed."

Silence descended again; the only sounds now were the slurping of coffee and the scraping of the chairs on the floor. Giannopoulos and Martin came shortly after and sat at the same table. I brought them two coffees.

"Sorry," Martin said. He'd not brought Bobby with him.

"She tried her best," Giannopoulos added.

I wished the men would start talking or playing games. Their silence and my own private knowledge of what had actually happened made me feel uneasy and exposed. The nets had been destroyed. I was sure no one would've bothered to notice whether one or two large holes had been cut into them. As far as the men knew, Kerryn had endangered her own life – had risked getting caught in the net herself – in her attempt to save Pavlos.

I ducked behind the bar and started fumbling through the money in the shoebox. It was a pittance, a few thousand drachmas by my estimation, though I didn't have the patience to actually count it. I was relieved to be out of sight of the fishermen, to have my face and shame hidden near the dirty floor behind the bar where I stayed for most of the day.

I arrived at the cove just as the dark edge of the setting sun began to slice through the mountain. Kerryn was sitting on the dock, legs crossed beneath her. She was staring at the sea and was utterly inert, no rocking or tapping, a sight of unquiet tranquility. I walked to the dock cautiously, treading as lightly as possible on the planks, feeling as if I no longer belonged here, as if I were trespassing. I sat next to her.

Seeing Kerryn, I had become aware of the cavity in my gut – my last meal had been more than twenty-four hours before – and the nervousness and unease that seemed to be trapped there. At the moment the sun sliced fully through the mountain and the darkness had raced out to the horizon, she spoke.

"What could I do?" Her voice was weak, the words breathy and unsure. "All I did was react. I didn't have time to think. I saw Pavlos jump in and swim over there, and he didn't come up. Yukon was already caught. Dolphins can only hold their breath for about fifteen minutes or so, that's all. I'd been waiting for Yukon... for a long time. And when Yukon stopped struggling... How could I know how long she'd been down there?"

"There was no way to know." I tried to speak with authority, to lend my voice the confidence that hers lacked.

"I had a second. A second. No time to think. Just react. Can you understand? I didn't have time to think, so I just, just... reached out to the thing I loved most."

The night before in my shack, tossing on the bed in the windless hours before dawn, anxious and unsettled, I knew that what Kerryn had done was challenge the basic hierarchy in our lives. For her, human life did not take precedence over all other forms. That was an unjust arrogance. For her, and her specifically, humans were greedy and predatory; they harbored evil, many of them. For those reasons, she didn't love Yukon for her human-like qualities; she did not project humanity on Yukon. No, she tried to meet Yukon on Yukon's level. To her, dolphins were artists, dreamers, musicians; they were faithful, friendly, loyal, honest and linked to a higher power.

A long time ago, Kerryn had chosen Yukon's love and affection over human love; now she had chosen Yukon's life over human life. In time, she had convinced me, as well, that dolphins were in every way equal to humans, if not superior. Still, out of what I can only term loyalty to my species, I'd have saved Pavlos first, instinctively. Just as instinctively, she had saved Yukon. The more I attempted to understand it, the more it seemed to slip away, to get further and further from the possibility of comprehension.

I placed my hands on Kerryn's shoulders and made small circles over her skin, trying to comfort her in some small way. The golden tan of her face and neck had turned to a burnt red, as if she'd developed a rash. As I massaged her shoulders, she made no motion whatsoever, neither resistance nor compliance. After a few minutes, she turned and looked at me with her large, deep eyes, swollen from her tears.

"How'd this happen?" she asked.

The blueness of the sea had been snapped away by nightfall. Kerryn sniffed, and then there were footsteps on the dock behind us. I turned to see Martin approaching.

"Funeral will be tomorrow at noon," he said. "Election is the day after that."

When neither of us responded, he turned and walked back down the dock, his feet treading solemnly on the planks. He had just stepped off the dock and onto the dirt when Kerryn spoke to me. I heard Martin stop and turn around.

"A dress," she whispered to me. "I need a dress and some shoes."

"Anythin' I can do?" Martin called.

When I repeated her request, he said that he would find them for her, that any one of the ladies would be proud to lend them, and that I could pick them up tomorrow morning at the taverna.

The entire island turned out for the funeral in an assemblage of black dresses and old black suits. There was a lot of crying about a boy who, in life, had attracted little attention. I saw Pavlos' mother for the first time, a short, elderly woman in widow garb with a ravage of white hair.

None of the men spoke to Kerryn, but they seemed to grant her the same deference as the mother. She was wearing the black dress with black shoes that I'd picked up at the taverna earlier in the day. The men and women seemed to take special notice of her and spoke in whispers whenever she came near. They saw her as the one who'd been right all along, who'd seen the danger of these nets long before anyone else.

The small rock church was located on the far corner of the village, facing the open sea. The congregation poured into the rear and side doors. They milled about and spoke in hushed tones as the ancient long-bearded priest mumbled prayers for the salvation of Pavlos' soul. Then the priest led us in a procession across the village, through a passageway that ran twenty meters above the dusty road. Six strong boys, including Pete, the young kid who had defended Pavlos on the soccer field, hoisted the coffin.

I stood next to Kerryn during the ceremony and, as we walked across the village, she tried not to cry. Out of the corner of my eye, I could see her lifting her head at regular intervals, relying on gravity to retain the tears. She shuffled along in a manner that was the direct opposite of her former way of striding proudly around the cove. Martin caught up with us during the procession.

"You did your best," he said to Kerryn. "Everyone knows that."

This confused Kerryn, and I realized that she'd no idea how the island thought of her. At that moment, she must've come to appreciate the enormity of the secret we held between us, for she turned and gave me a long, unblinking look. As I stared back, she must've understood that no one but we two would ever know what happened in the cove that morning. And she surely recognized, as I did, the burden that knowledge would impose.

In the cemetery, we gathered around the coffin. As the priest said the last few prayers, memories of Pavlos flooded back to me, and I realized I had spent the funeral thinking of Kerryn, not Pavlos. But now I recalled the lonely outcast at the soccer games, the budding artist who viewed the world in exotic proportions, his glorified impression of Americky; I remembered him placing his chin on the bar and following me around the taverna with his eyes, drinking screw-ups, and then coming to the cove and playing with Yukon and being, for those fleeting moments, included. Throughout all these thoughts, I was haunted by his last few moments, of what must have run through his head in his final breaths, when Kerryn was cutting Yukon free. I could only hope that he was too panicked to realize what was happening. I scolded myself for discarding Pavlos' napkins so easily.

A slight breeze slipped through the trees, and I bowed my head to say a prayer. But it was as if I'd forgotten how. I noticed the crimson clay beneath my feet and how small and simple were the tombstones, randomly scattered. I began to count them. It was important to know how many others he would be joining in this simple plot. Forty two. As if only forty-two others had ever died on the island – so few it appeared that death came only by accident here.

There was to be a gathering at someone's house after the ceremony, and the group was herded in that direction. Kerryn and I fell behind and let them pass us. We would not attend. When I watched the crowd walk up the hill, I was struck by one image: Papakakis alone, a pariah the day before the election. Even his own men kept a safe distance from him and, as long as I watched, nobody spoke to him. I was pleased to see this. He hadn't intended for this to happen, hadn't wanted Pavlos to die. But that didn't matter now, and I hoped it didn't matter to the fishermen.

Kerryn and I turned the other way and walked back to the cove. As we broke through the tunnel of trees and wordlessly went to our separate shacks, I tried to convince myself that it wasn't her fault – that no one should be asked to perform that sort of triage. She'd celebrated Yukon's intellectual and emotional gifts and elevated her to a position that was equal to our own. As far as I could tell, she was entirely right to do so. But in this tiny world of scarcity, that moral position had come at a price. That the price was so high was not her fault. It was not a defect in her that took Pavlos' life, but rather a defect in this small and merciless trap of a planet, which pitted all its creatures against one another in an unceasing battle for survival.

19

The next morning, I left for work without seeing Kerryn. There was no noise or other sign of life in her shack, but I knew she was there. I'd slept fitfully when I managed to sleep at all in the last few nights, snapping upright at a rustle in the trees, a squawk from a lone bird, the sudden lapping of water onto the shore, the sea licking its wounds. If Kerryn had left, I'd have heard that too.

I hadn't seen Yukon since she'd been freed from the net. I hadn't seen her swim away that day either, but I felt sure she hadn't returned to the cove. There was no way she couldn't have sensed what had happened to Pavlos, and what had nearly happened to her. Like any intelligent creature, she'd choose to avoid the area.

The shame and sadness hadn't diminished with the passing days. During those fitful nights, I'd developed the habit of pacing, counting my steps and refusing to return to bed until I'd walked five hundred times across the room, taking five steps each pass. I tried to use the counting as a source of distraction, but it did little good. In the midst of these midnight walks, the smirking man returned, repeating again and again that I could leave this dying island, that there was nothing between Kerryn and me but a few nights of fun, that

Pavlos had been an unhappy kid to begin with. Only this time, a part of me sensed that there was something larger that I needed to grasp, that there was something within me that I hadn't yet uncovered with my steps.

As I made my way to the village, I began to understand that, at the very least, I'd put some distance between the smirking man and the man I wanted to be. That I'd become increasingly aware of his presence and this awareness gave me a power over him I'd not had before.

Along with this awareness came the realization that any ability I may have gained in this regard – the ability to hold off the smirking man – was offset by the loss of the promise of redemption, which had been abandoned in the cove along with Pavlos. His death removed any sense of purpose or plan, merely reinforced the truth that we reside on the dark side of this planet, seeing and believing in, but never able to quite step into the warmth and light, existing always in shadows and shades. If, before, I believed that the worst of people and events were for a reason, I couldn't believe that anymore. I didn't believe in anything anymore. The pilgrimage that I'd fooled myself into believing I was making was over, had perhaps never even begun.

I grew tired. I felt like I'd been walking forever. I looked down at the crystal sea glistening below me, to the imposing blueness of the sky, to the mountain stretching sternly toward the heavens, and I could see beauty in none of it.

The taverna was open when I arrived, and I soon found out why: Mr. Giorgos had come back for the election, which was this very day. I'd forgotten all about it.

"Didn't think I'd come back, did you?" Mr. Giorgos said to me. "Neither did I. Those Spanish women can do things…" He brought two fingers to his lips and kissed them. "They will be there when I go back. And I wanted to be here for Kostas, the idiot."

The place was more crowded than ever before. There were twenty or more people I'd never seen before. All the tables were full. Everyone seemed to know one another, though a lot of the newcomers were obviously out of place – their shiny shoes, even if dusted over, gave them away. There was a man with finely shaped blow-dried hair and creased pants. Another man's designer watch flashed striped reflections against the wall. All the young men were more affluent and worldly than their fishermen fathers. Some spoke to me in clipped and proper English; others had the refined continental manners of aristocrats, too polite and gentle to ever have worked the sea. There were a few young women also, quite unlike the island women; modern women, these were, stronger, well dressed, independent, and unafraid to occupy the taverna.

"We've been on Skopiathos for two days now," the man with the blow dried hair told me, "been staying at my sister's there. Nice to come back to the islands every once in a while. Haven't seen you before? American? Can you vote?"

Another man in a suit about forty years old told me he was on vacation. "Anything I can do for old Kostas Giannopoulos. A good man. Tell me, do you think the dollar is over-valued?"

A woman from Salonika asked, "What's a man like you doing here? Are you crazy, or some sort of criminal?"

These strange, energetic people made me fretful and uncomfortable. I tried to elude them as best I could, but the taverna proved too small. They were unavoidable and embodied everything the island would no longer be – neither simple nor traditional nor isolated. They provided further evidence that despite Kerryn's words to the contrary, the outside world still existed, would always exist, and would always intrude. As these outsiders packed themselves between the four walls, I had to go outside. I couldn't stand the ready-made small talk, the plentiful slaps on the back, the jubilant drinking.

On the doorstep of the taverna, I chewed on a piece of grass. Everything seemed transformed as I gazed at the dirt of the empty soccer field, the rudimentary buildings of the harbor, the wooden fishing boats seemingly no more than toys and at all the old, old people. It had all turned septic. What was once the refreshing isolation now seemed like an unbearable remoteness, the astute simplicity of the inhabitants had become naive provincialism; the heat (though the weather was cooling) was an inescapable sauna; the food as unimaginative as a daily bowl of rice.

With this mindset, I watched a thick-necked, bald, middle-aged man in a buttoned white shirt and loose tie as he sat at a table just outside the general store. There were two other men there, Harry and a man from Papakakis' taverna. They stood at opposite sides of the table. Paper ballots and a locked metal box lay side by side in the middle.

Giannopoulos came out and stood next to me. His presence made me feel awkward until I realized he'd no intention of talking to me. He had a notebook in his hand and was staring at the voting table. I looked across the way and saw Papakakis doing the same thing.

Pavlos' mother was the first person to approach the thick-necked man. She said her name and received a ballot and an envelope. The other men checked her name off a computer printout – a bold assault of New World technology. With her ballot, she went to Harry who pointed to a name on the ballot. The respective taverna representatives, I understood, were to point to the name of the proper candidate for the voters who couldn't read. She then disappeared into the store. She returned with the sealed envelope and stuffed it into the box. This was the honorable process.

After voting, Pavlos' mother came toward our taverna and went to Giannopoulos. Politely, he stepped out to meet her and they embraced on the dusty road before she disappeared into a pathway in the village. As the hours crawled by, almost every single one of the fishermen walked over to Giannopoulos after voting and gravely shook his hand. At first, I took this as an island custom, a form of good sportsmanship, having to do with being *filotimo*. But by mid-afternoon it dawned on me that none of our fishermen had gone to shake Papakakis' hand.

"Don't tell me," I said as I slid up next to Martin.

"I won't then." Bobby was draped over Martin's left hand and lifted his head when Martin spoke. He sniffed the air, then licked his nose, as if he, too, didn't like the smell of all these *xenoi*, these foreigners. I smiled for the first time since Pavlos' death.

"Is it possible?" I said. It was incredible. "He won, didn't he? Giannopoulos won."

"If Bobby knew how to bark, he would."

The voting ended at sundown, with the arrival of the ferry. The voting table was quickly put away by the thick-necked man, and he headed to the ferry with the ballot box tucked under his arm.

At the taverna, Giannopoulos had begun to address the crowd, "We will have to wait for the official results tomorrow, but we have won this election, I believe. If this is the case, I will dedicate myself to the memory of Pavlos and my father. I will try to preserve this island as they knew it and as it should be. No one will get rich, and we will be what many people consider poor. But we will take care of each other, simple as that. Simple as that."

"Do you think he can really keep the island the way it is?" I asked Martin.

"I think he'll try."

"Think that's wise?" The words were out of my mouth before I thought about them.

Martin was quick: "CIA, I don't think anythin' is wise."

Kerryn knocked on my door the next morning. She stood outside my shack, blocking the rising sun. For the first time since I'd known her, she seemed ill at ease with herself, unsure of what she should say, or how to say it. I invited her inside, but she didn't move. She responded with an audible breath, a release of sorts in which her deep eyes, midnight black with the white sun behind her, transformed into pools of tears.

"It's okay," I said. She stepped forward and together we fell to the ground. She buried her head in my neck and gasped words through her tears that I couldn't quite understand.

I could find nothing to comfort her. My mind conceived only trite utterances – he's in a better place, give it time, it wasn't your fault – which I resisted speaking. Then I wanted to tell her that her sadness might just as well be rage, as mine was. Not just at Papakakis, or the fishermen, or the Athenians and other outsiders who sponsored their activities, but at ourselves and this tiny trap of a world. Perhaps Kerryn was right. Perhaps we'd all gone wrong when, before history began, we chose our murderous agricultural destiny and began tilling this endlessly abundant garden of ours for no better reason than we didn't know what we had – and wanted more. Perhaps we were indeed the cursed children of Cain, our gifts unwanted, our fate foretold.

For more than an hour, Kerryn leaned against my chest, her eyes closed, sobbing. I held her until she became motionless, until she had cried herself out and was without energy.

In time, she forced herself to speak: Was I wrong? Am I evil?".

She asked two questions, I answered the second one.

"No. No, of course not."

"I'm just so sorry. I'm sorry for Pavlos… sorry for you, sorry for me. I just want to sleep. I need to sleep for a long time. But I can't. What am I supposed to do? How can I prevent it from destroying everything?"

I looked into her wounded face, her dark eyes bloodshot and her cheeks stained with tears and had no answer. I had nothing to say at all.

20

The taverna buzzed with anticipation the next afternoon. Everyone was certain that Giannopoulos had won, but there was still anxiety. The election no longer mattered to me, except as a reprisal for what Papakakis had done. Who had actually placed the nets in the cove? It was a question never answered, because it was a question never asked. Papakakis had ordered them, of that I was certain, though he'd not intended for Pavlos to die. And since nothing would bring Pavlos back, what did it matter?

Papakakis was conspicuously absent when the ferry arrived. He must've known better than anyone that the election was lost. I'd not seen or heard from him since election day, and even then, by late afternoon, he had the look of a beaten man.

The ferry arrived just before sundown and was met by the large crowd that had gathered on the dusty road. A few anonymous people disembarked first, fishermen and old ladies with torn shirts and ragged bags. The crowd moved aside to let them pass, and when they did, Giannopoulos stepped forward. He cut through the crowd as if entering a boxing ring, sprightly and aggressive, a bright smile on his face. Murmurs scuttled through the crowd and scattered bits of applause broke out as he ascended the ramp. Giannopoulos made no acknowledgment but simply faced the ferry and waited.

Nothing happened for a long moment, as we waited for the election official. Everyone was holding their breath. You could hear the water's unsteady slapping against the side of the ferry.

There was a collective exhale when the thick-necked man in a white shirt and fat yellow tie stepped off the ferry. Giannopoulos offered his hand and helped him from the boat. The thick-necked man was carrying a black briefcase and, as he hopped on the dock, his bright tie flew over his shoulder. Giannopoulos politely returned it to the proper position.

The two men strolled leisurely into the village. At the general store, Giannopoulos went inside and came out with a thin, rickety chair. The man sat down and put the briefcase on his lap. The crowd had followed and was gathered around. He took a set of keys out of his pocket and opened the two locks on the case. With as much pomposity as he could muster, he removed a sealed folder.

The tail end of the sun was visible over the houses, and the village smelled of sweat and diesel from the ferry. The man started with a brief run-down of the election rules, and how they counted the votes, and a bunch of other official nonsense. He concluded by saying that he was satisfied that the election itself and the tabulation of the votes was, in his opinion, fair.

"And the Mayor is…" he hesitated and the crowd lunged forward "…Kostas Giannopoulos with –"

Nobody heard anything further. A quick *whoop* went up and was followed by a swelling of cheers. But just as quickly they stopped – when, almost at once, the villagers realized that what had brought about this victory was nothing to celebrate.

I was relieved more than anything else, glad that Giannopoulos would get his chance. At this time, I felt something funny on my leg and looked down to see Bobby licking me.

"The man deserves it," Martin said.

We both looked back at the subdued celebration, which consisted primarily of long handshakes and quick hugs. Then there was a general milling around, as if the people were looking for something they had lost. They couldn't quite celebrate, but neither could they mourn, and so they were left with nothing to do. In almost no time, the flustered crowd had migrated back up the passageways to their homes, vanishing into the village, and leaving only two pale foreigners – an Irishman and an American – and the castaway puppy standing off to the side.

Giannopoulos, too, was left in the middle of the road. He noticed us and walked over, extending his hand first to Martin and then to me.

"I thought it would feel better than this," Giannopoulos said. He paused and eyed Martin slyly before adding, "Don't say it."

"What?" Martin responded.

"Anything."

"Kostas, I'm hurt. Do you possibly think I'd take your great, swollen moment and deflate it by mentionin' how every victory is another's loss and –"

"– Shut up, my friend." Giannopoulos said. "Especially when I might finally be able to do the island some good. It's funny; all my life was aimed at this moment. I gave up everything. And now that it's here..." He spun and took in the village behind us, the tiny houses jutting up from the hill, the stores and two tavernas on the dusty road, the fishing boats in the harbor. "It isn't much. It's almost nothing at all."

His disappointment was palpable, as if he had just discovered how very small the island really was.

"Your father would be proud," I said.

"Yes," he replied, without enthusiasm.

Martin, too, glanced at the village, then put his arm around Giannopoulos' shoulder. "Feckin' hell, Kostas, I like this place as well as any other." He scooped up Bobby from the ground. "The idea of tryin' to preserve it like it is, that's somethin'. Not the actual doin' of it, of course, that's terrible shite... but the *idea* of preservin' it, that's good. Make sense? I don't care. Can I buy us all twenty drinks?"

Giannopoulos put his arm around Martin's shoulder and mine and pushed us all toward the taverna. "Come, my friends. Let's have twenty drinks." We started to the taverna like that, with the mayor's arms linked across our shoulders.

The taverna appeared to have shrunk, too. It wasn't much bigger than my shack and smelled of stale fish and alcohol. I pulled out a bottle of Jack Daniel's and put it on a table with three glasses. It wasn't genuine Jack Daniel's, of course, but a cheap imitation that would leave us all with terrible hangovers.

We sat at the table with our knees knocking one another – Martin kept his hurt leg off to the side – and talked of many things. Giannopoulos told us how his father had tried to start a library one summer, donating books to teach the men and women to read. Only the winter that year was long and cold, and soon they were indeed judging every book by its cover as they were burning them for heat.

As we were drinking our fourth and fifth glasses of whiskey, Martin told us how he'd lived his entire life to get the British out of Ireland, how he was proud of his courage and fortitude but not of all things he'd done. "Terrible things," he said. Then, one day, he'd discovered that the people in the South of Ireland didn't seem to care as much about reuniting the island as he thought, that most of them had gone on with their own lives. And he realized he'd been fighting, in part, for something in his own mind.

He took a swig of whiskey and slowly pulled up his pants leg, exposing his disfigured kneecap. He pounded it hard with his fist. I couldn't help but gasp.

"Did this to my own damn self, believe it or not," he said. "Sat in a stolen car outside the hospital and pulled the feckin' trigger. Wanted to feel it and wanted out, and this was one way to do it. Hurt more than you can imagine, and my screams brought the doctors out. When they fixed me up, the bloody Brits questioned me for two weeks, one of them smackin' my knee with his gun when he didn't feel my answers were right. Hurt like the devil's hemorrhoided arse, but I said nothin'. What I did was realize those bastards were just like me, almost the same age, could've even been my mates, if they hadn't been born over the line. We told jokes to each other at one point, we did. We laughed together, then they got back to me and my knee. How 'bout that for shite?"

He gulped down the last of the whiskey, winked, and started to sing:

"As back through the glen, I rode again, my heart with grief was sore. For I parted then with valiant men, whom I shall see no more…"

As the imitation whiskey warmed my body, I understood that I, too, was with valiant men, men who engaged the right-eous battle for its own sake, superior to me in so many ways that it sent my drunken mind reeling. Yet, we three men, as opposite as we were, could this night be called friends. If we had only our disappointments in common – in our victories, our losses, ourselves – this was, at least, something we shared.

21

I woke up late, hung-over, and went for a swim to clear my head. At the dock, I saw Kerryn in the water with Yukon. I was surprised that Yukon was there – it was the first I'd seen her since the tragedy – but I shouldn't have been. Kerryn needed Yukon now more than ever. They weren't swimming together, and there was a hesitancy in the small repetitive loops Yukon formed around Kerryn. Kerryn was dipping her head in the water and lifting it out slowly, time and again. Eventually, she tired of this and sat on the dock. I sat next to her. The dock was baking in the midday sun, and I had to shift my weight on my thighs to keep them from burning.

"Haven't seen Yukon for a while," I said.

"Right," she said and then, "go, Yukon. Until tomorrow."

We watched Yukon's dorsal fin disappear under the water. A few moments later, it emerged near the edge of the cove and then disappeared again. Kerryn put her hands over her eyes and held them there. Her body, clothed in jean shorts and bikini top, rocked back and forth. I wrapped her in my arms and held her still.

The sun burned as ruthlessly as it had all summer. The sea in the cove glimmered, reflected and danced in thick ripples. Kerryn began to tremble. I kissed her, hard, clapping my mouth on hers. A supplicant to my wishes, she went limp in my arms. I kissed her again, hard.

"Do it," she whispered.

All at once, and for reasons beyond my understanding, I was overcome. I pressed her down to the dock and rolled on top of her. The dock had been broiling in the sun and mercilessly burned my knees and feet and hands. I could only imagine what it was doing to Kerryn's back. I stripped off her shorts and top. She whimpered as the newly exposed skin touched the fiery wood planks.

"Do it," she said again.

She pulled me into her with all her strength. Then we were gasping and trying to get farther and farther away from ourselves, trying to get farther inside the other. I wanted to possess her and own her and tear her apart. Someone between the smirking man and someone else, I was trying to hurt her and be hurt, or to please her and be pleased, but most of all just going deeper, deeper, trying to dig something out of her or force something out of me, some vile remnant, or some forgotten artifact of our love, digging for Pavlos himself and for everything that might've been... But the harsh scorching of the dock beneath us began to fade, and as it did, something greater went with it. When we finally rolled apart, we were further estranged than ever.

As the wood seared my back, I stared into the blinding brightness of the sun. I was bitter. I felt betrayed, by Kerryn, by myself, and by the island. I'd been searching for a way to forgive myself, to re-enter the world as a new man, redeemed and blessed, as I'd been promised. Suddenly, I understood what this burning, this digging had been about. The death of Pavlos had validated the smirking man. The death of Pavlos justified a life of domination and possession and grabbiness. I may not be the smirking man anymore, I may have managed to banish him in some way, but he'd won. When Pavlos died, the smirking man won.

"I'm sorry," I said, whether to her or to me, I wasn't entirely sure. "Kerryn, I am so sorry."

As I spoke those words, something in me began to melt. It was as if my emotions had been trapped within ice and suddenly they began to liquefy and flow, one joining into the other and forming an unstoppable current of shame and fear and remorse and anger that sluiced through my veins. I looked at Kerryn and then rose and went to my shack. I fell into bed and remained there, as if there were no bones, no structure in my body.

The next day, I arrived in the village just as the ferry was preparing to depart, grinding up the anchor it had dropped. The heavy chain noisily clattered back into the bow until the anchor emerged from the water, carrying with it a mass of black dirt that fell off in large, wet chunks and splashed back to the water. The ferry was pulling away from the harbor now, leaving a thick streak of blue tinged water in its wake. I envied the passengers taking their seats, no matter where they were going.

That afternoon I quit my job at the taverna. Now that Mr. Giorgos had returned, I wasn't needed anymore anyway. With only a hint of a smile, he asked if I'd like a recommendation for my next job. He also told me that from now on all my drinks were free, though added that if I drank too much, I wouldn't get a good recommendation. I said I'd keep that in mind and poured myself a large ouzo.

I rolled the clear, aromatic liquid around in the glass and slowly added water. I was down to nothing; I'd no savings, no job, and no prospects. I was poorer than the poor fishermen who surrounded me and who'd once again accepted me. Over the next few hours, they invited me into their gossip and card games. Though I didn't care if I won or lost, or who'd done what to whom, I played cards to pass the time and gossiped about things I knew nothing about.

Mr. Giorgos had discovered a new drink in Spain and was eager to introduce it to the men at the taverna. You filled a shot glass with tequila and ginger ale and covered it with a handkerchief. After shaking it, you slammed it down on the table and drank it as it fizzed. He called it a *taka-taka*.

Mr. Giorgos placed the combustible mixture in front of Martin and Harry and Ari and Yannis the Red and me and the rest of them. We had to cover the glasses with whatever we had, our hands or napkins or shirts, then smash them to the table and drink. It was more of a ritual than anything else, and a lot of trouble at that, but the taverna took to it. The men kept Mr. Giorgos busy pouring the drinks. Eventually, I helped him out by following him around the room, pouring the ginger ale after he poured the tequila.

Around dusk, some of the fishermen from the other taverna came to our side of the village. The former enemies entered cautiously, nodded politely and sat down at a table. Mr. Giorgos wasted no time in getting them drinking *taka-takas*. But they sat alone, as intruders, smoking, sweating and drinking by themselves. After a time, Giannopoulos entered the room. He spotted the men instantly, smiled and sat down with them. Together they smacked their drinks on the table and kicked them back, laughing, singing and belching.

As I sat in the corner of the taverna, Martin came over and quietly said he shouldn't have mentioned those things the other night, and he hoped I'd forget.

"What things?" I said and asked Martin something that had been bothering me all summer. It was about the fires on the mountain, how they got started and why nobody ever seemed to care.

"They just start," he said. "Can't prevent them, and so they just burn and burn. All you can do is keep puttin' them out. Keep puttin' them out."

Martin and I looked at each other strangely, oddly, as if we were seeing each other for the first time. And then, as if on cue, we covered our glasses, smashed them to the table and gulped them down.

❧

In the morning, I looked out of my shack and saw Kerryn sitting like a statue on the dock. Her legs were crossed beneath her, and she was staring at the open sea. I approached and sat down next to her. What had happened between us the last time on the dock was something neither of us wanted to discuss, and so we sat next to each other like strangers in a foreign airport, speaking different languages, held together by nothing more than being in the same place at the same time.

I recalled that night in the sanctuary, the bottle cap moon and prism rainbow, with Yukon at my feet and Kerryn in my arms. For the first time in my life, I'd loved, truly loved. I'd been making love to more than just Kerryn that night; she was a conduit into which I injected my immense gratitude for life itself, for living, for feeling. But I could see that I'd been fooled, deluded by the moon and sea and circumstances. The decision she'd made under the water had thrown me back to the hard understanding that such acceptance and surrender is an aberration. That vulnerabilities and love and generosity are, for any length of time, unsustainable.

The day was muggy, but in the breeze that floated over the water there was an edge, a distinct coolness that presaged the end of the summer. A flock of large black birds flew overhead, a sign of early migration. They flew in the large 'V' shape that broke the wind for the weaker ones in the rear who struggled to keep up, the strongest ones alternating in the wearying lead.

I stared at the cove, trying to get accustomed to the fact that it was no longer ours. That it never was. Just a simple cove in the Aegean, it was nothing more than that – a pleasant place we had borrowed and had to return.

"Will you go?" I asked her.

Yukon arrived and started making slow circles beneath us in the water.

"I don't know," she said.

"And Yukon?"

"We just have to find a place, somewhere…"

But I knew that every cove would be the same. The world would always prove too small, abundant only in its scarcity. There were too many of us, and we all wanted too much, and so we encroached and abandoned each other with a smirking cruelty. Kerryn and Yukon would never find that place – it was an illusion. Any gulf or bay or cove they might find – if they ever found another – would be just another place in another sea belonging to people and powers greater than both of them.

"But it doesn't exist," I said. "Have you thought of that? Have you even considered that? That garden. It doesn't exist."

"Yes, it does." The words were firm, determined.

Didn't she understand? Couldn't I make it clear to her that there was no place like the one she wanted? Couldn't she see that? I was a faithless former pilgrim, and her conviction infuriated me.

"I'm leaving," I blurted.

She did not respond for some time and then said, "I know you can't live with me. I can't live with myself. But I'm asking you to, anyway."

I looked away, stunned. She had no right to make such a request. I thought it best to cut it off as quickly as possible. "Every time we looked at each other, we would be reminded of what happened. Right or wrong, doesn't matter. We'd know. If we're apart, maybe we can manage to move on. And that's the important thing. That's always the important thing."

"There's a place," she insisted.

I hugged her, and as every part of my body clamored for her, every construct in my mind told me I had to leave. She reached over and held me – held me until I gathered myself enough to walk away. I walked down the dock and couldn't prevent myself from looking back when I reached the end. Slow moving clouds cast giant gray shadows on the earth, and the sea rippled in the cooling breeze. On the edge of the dock, Kerryn's back was bright red, scorched and blistered from the day before. She was staring at Yukon, calling to her, and she was thin and strong and naked and golden and alone.

22

Here is a shameful thing that I did.

I borrowed a fishing boat and, with Martin, circled the island until we found steep cliffs of white rock. There, I jumped out of the boat and began to swim the coast, investigating every hole or cave or cavern that looked big enough to fit a man, a woman, and a dolphin. I'd been in the water for more than an hour when I found it. It was unmistakable, the jagged rocks guarding the entrance, the inverted cone above me. It was very different in the daytime, tiny and damp and barren. When I saw a rusted beer can on the sand, I felt better about what I was about to do.

I swam back to the boat, grabbed a sack and returned. Then I looked around, up through the funnel and back toward the sea, to make sure no one was looking, and placed the small, timeless Cycladic beauty into the sack. I swam back to the boat knowing I was holding onto something more valuable than I'd ever hold again. It was priceless, and I was rich. I could roam the world without constraint, running forever.

As I climbed in the boat, Martin looked at me, at the sack, then back at me, but said nothing. I clasped the sack, now heavy, wet and angular, to my chest. We returned to the harbor without a word and went our separate ways. The trip was never mentioned again.

I hid the Cycladic woman in my shack and spent the next day and night at the taverna, drinking *taka-taka*s and saying my good-byes to Martin, Mr. Giorgos, Harry, Ari and the other fishermen. Nobody seemed surprised that I was leaving, and they all wished me well. Martin said Bobby would miss me and lifted him so he could lick me across the mouth. After he put Bobby down, Martin bear-hugged me, like a Greek, and kissed me on both cheeks, like a Greek. Without any worthless promises to call or write, we said good-bye affectionately and for the last time.

When I returned to the cove that night, I threw all my things including the Cycladic beauty into the duffel bag. These things were, literally, everything I owned in the world. As I tried to sleep, I tuned into the sounds around me, the crickets, the wind, the trees, the sea. These were sounds that had outlasted all of mankind's dreams and pilgrimages. These sounds held a strength and permanence in a breakable and transient world. For eons, this was the way the cove must have sounded, and perhaps with luck, unimaginable luck, it would go on sounding this way for eons more.

I stared at the ceiling and thought that each of us had our own unshakable truths that we cherished and from which most other thoughts and emotions arised. My own truths were passionless and simple: this world was cruel and predatory; human greed and selfishness were appropriate, even necessary responses; and redemption was the delusion of fools. I thought I knew Kerryn's truths as well: despite all she'd been through, she believed this world to be abundant and benevolent, a manifest and shining sanctuary meant to be shared by all its sentient creatures.

I wondered if we were both wrong... if we were both right.

In the morning, I didn't leave my shack right away but waited until mid-afternoon to avoid Kerryn and another wretched good-bye. In a final display of Greek hospitality, Ari and Harry had agreed to drive me to the village. In fact, they'd insisted. I walked past Kerryn's shack quickly. There was a small pile outside: a pencil, a pair of shorts, a coffee cup. So, soon, she would have nothing at all. I walked through the tunnel of trees with my duffel bag without looking back and waited outside for the rusted blue Fiat to arrive. My trip from the cove ended as it had begun, with Ari's scratchy voice:

"*En-ah . . . thee-oh . . . tree-ah.*"

At the taverna, Mr. Giorgos tried to talk me into staying another month or two. He said he'd heard of a notorious Bulgarian resort on the Black Sea and needed me to run the taverna.

"The women there," Mr. Giorgos told me, "they are crazy and they drink like Russians. They know old Stalinist sex secrets that make men wild. You stay here, and I can go there."

But I'd already bought a ticket for the ferry at the general store, paying the young girl with a bill featuring Giannopoulos as a donkey. When the ferry arrived, Mr. Giorgos gave me twenty thousand drachmas for nothing and told me there'd always be a job waiting for me. I threw my duffel bag over my shoulder and headed to the pier.

As I climbed the metal ramp, I saw Giannopoulos talking to the ferry captain. The new mayor saluted me and smiled. I smiled and saluted him back, proudly, the way I imagined a CIA agent would do, with my right hand angled against a sweaty brow. As the lines were thrown from the dock, I felt I'd left something undone and should go back. I resisted the tug of these feelings, knowing that, for my own good, I must defy them. As the ferry backed out of the harbor, I thought of Kerryn, and how I'd loved her, and did nothing, and how she would live somewhere else without me, without anyone, abandoned again. And I did nothing.

I turned to look back at the island, at the purity of the white houses against the clear blue sea, at the harsh barren landscape, at the fishing boats and the fading cries of the fishing men in the untidy harbor, at the general store and the two tavernas, all illuminated by the bright, wide sun. I tried hard to look at it as if for the first time, to study the picture objectively, before the image would be forever distorted in my mind by memories and the unfolding of time. I'd come to terms with the smirking man inside me perhaps, but the island was largely leaving me as it had found me: without markings, without bearings.

Another fire had started on the mountain. Like God descended it brightly burned – yellow, white and red flames reaching for the sky, threatening to destroy everything. The flames, of course, would be ignored by the inhabitants. The planes would come eventually, but who really cared? Not me, not them, not anyone.

I grew weary as the distance from the island increased and sat down on a bench, next to the feet of an old sleeping fisherman, gray matted hair, face lined with the creases of age, the familiar smell of old fish and oil rising from his clothes. The fisherman slept quietly and contentedly, resembling the reclining Buddha.

I was numb and empty. Behind me, on the fiery island that I was leaving forever, Yukon swam in the blue sea with Kerryn. And they swam without me. What did it all mean? Could it mean nothing at all? How is a person, any person, supposed to combat the regret and despair that loiters in the soul?

Suddenly, from nowhere, I felt that time – *time* – was passing rapidly, that it was being wasted. This confused me.

How could time be wasting if I'd nowhere to go and nothing to do? Time for what? But the feeling was there, undeniably. I wished the ferry would go faster.

The island was going now, the tip of the mountain rounding into the sea. I looked at the sleeping fisherman and thought that, if nothing else, the island had been evidence of this: nothing that really matters is ever left behind, nothing is ever found. Invoking irredeemable choices, the netting of our existence is inescapable, and we are caught in it, forced to rebel against it in our very first and last steps, to free ourselves and find someplace...

But it doesn't exist.

Yes, it does.

What kept her convinced despite such overwhelming evidence to the contrary? It could only be that Kerryn possessed an immense reserve of hope – and perhaps this was the final possession she'd been trying to get down to all along. If she gave away everything else that is all she would be left with, and it would fill her life. In this regard she was different from me, different from anyone, in her superior capacity for hope.

And hope may be the only remedy for regret.

The ferry was now surrounded by the sea on all sides. No sight of land in any direction. Kerryn. *If you let go of what holds you down, you can float; you can fly.* How could I have known that unless she told me? How could I have known about floating and flying – that floating and flying is easy, merely a matter of getting rid of that which keeps you down? That you can harness the yearning to pull you up, up, up?

As if I'd been hit by the weight of this realization, my head snapped back. I spotted a fishing boat veering off to avoid the wake from the ferry and recognized some of the men. They weren't people I knew. They were from the other taverna, the former enemy, but that didn't matter. They would be *filotimo*;

I could count on that. I grabbed my duffel bag and hugged it firmly. Then I winked good-bye to the sleeping Buddha-fisherman and flung myself over the side.

"*Opah!*"

The ferry steamed off; no one had noticed me. Only the fishermen in the boat saw me. They yelled and turned in my direction.

I gave myself up to the water, twisting and bobbing. The duffel bag began to sink and pull me down. I hesitated – it contained everything I had in the world – it held the Cycladic beauty, the most perfect and valuable object I'd ever possess.

And I let her go.

It was easy. I didn't need her. I didn't need any of it.

All I had to do was let go.

The wake from the ferry bounced me high and then swallowed me. When I emerged, out of breath, coughing, gasping, my chest heaving desperately, I was tossed again and lost all sense of direction, inhaling a mouthful of water. It was in my lungs, my eyes, my nose. I didn't know how much longer I could hold out –

But no matter, the fishermen's boat had arrived.

ACKNOWLEDGMENTS

For their love and support:

My mother and father, Betty and Albert Hogan
John Hogan
Betsy and Warren Johnston, Nancy and Al Perna, Jane and
Bill Crooks
Nikos and Niki Papaioannou, Nina Papaioannou, Yanna
Papaioannou
&
Ismini, Jack and Nikolas,
who make it all worthwhile

Special thanks:

Jerry Guardino
Frank D'Angeli
Linda Forrester
Laurence O'Bryan
&
Svetlana Pironko,
who made it all possible

ABOUT THE AUTHOR

David Hogan is the author of a number of screen and stage plays. His stage plays include the NPI award-winning *Capital, Samoan America, Fore,* and *No Sit – No Stand – No Lie,* which opened the 'Resilience of the Spirit' Human Rights Festival. His screenplays, which have been optioned and sold, include *The Tractor King, Fear the Meat, Free Radical* and *Stranded.*

A dual citizen of the US and Ireland, David lived and worked in Greece for a number of years. He currently resides in Southern California where he is an avid surfer.

To learn more about David, visit *http://davidhoganwriter. com* and w*ww.betimesbooks.com*

Made in the USA
San Bernardino, CA
15 November 2013